Mary Downing Hahn

The Girl in the Locked Room

A Ghost Story

Houghton Mifflin Harcourt
Boston   New York

hmhbooks.com

The text was set in Janson MT Std.

The Library of Congress has cataloged the hardcover edition as follows:
Names: Hahn, Mary Downing, author.
Title: The girl in the locked room : a ghost story / Mary Downing Hahn.
Description: Boston ; New York : Clarion Books, Houghton Mifflin Harcourt,
[2018] | Summary: Told in two voices, Jules, whose father is restoring an
abandoned house, and a girl who lived there a century before begin to
communicate and slowly, the girl's tragic story is revealed.
Identifiers: LCCN 2018006980 |
Subjects: | CYAC: Ghosts—Fiction. | Friendship—Fiction. |
Extrasensory perception—Fiction. | Fate and fatalism—Fiction. |
Haunted houses—Fiction. | Family life—Virginia—Fiction. | Virginia—Fiction. |
BISAC: JUVENILE FICTION / Social Issues / Friendship. |
JUVENILE FICTION /
Girls & Women.
Classification: LCC PZ7.H1256 Gir 2018 | DDC [Fic]—dc23
LC record available at https://lccn.loc.gov/2018006980

ISBN: 978-1-328-85092-8 hardcover
ISBN: 978-0-358-09755-6 paperback

Printed in the United States of America
DOC 10 9 8 7 6 5 4
4500810103

For my young cousin, Kate,
and my great-nieces, Ava and Charlotte

The Girl

The girl is alone in the locked room. At first, she writes the day of the week, the month, and the year on a wall. She means to keep a record of her time in the room, but after a while she begins skipping a day or several days. Soon, days, months, and years become a meaningless jumble. She forgets her birthday. And then her name.

But what does it matter? No one comes to visit, no one asks her name, no one asks how old she is.

At first, the room seems large, but soon it shrinks—or seems to. It becomes a prison. The key disappeared long ago. No matter—she's afraid to leave. They're waiting for her to open the door. She feels their presence, faint in the daytime but solid and loud at night. Their boots storm up the steps. They hammer on the door. They yell for her to come out.

But how can she? The door is locked from the outside. Even if she wanted to, she could not obey their commands. She huddles in the shadows, her eyes closed, her fingers in her ears, and waits for them to leave.

The trouble is, they always come back. Not every night, but often enough that she always waits to hear their horses gallop toward the house, to hear their boots on the stairs, to hear their fists on her door.

She used to know who they were and why they came, but now she knows only that they are bad men who will hurt her if they find her. They say they won't, but she doesn't believe them.

So she huddles in the wardrobe, under a pile of old dresses, and doesn't move until she hears their horses gallop away.

Every morning, the girl looks at a date written on the wall—June 1, 1889. She doesn't remember why she wrote the date or what happened that day. Indeed, she isn't even sure she wrote it. Maybe someone else, some other girl, was here once. Maybe that girl wrote the date.

Someone, perhaps that other girl, certainly not herself, drew pictures on the wall. They tell a story, a terrible story. The story frightens her. It makes her cry sometimes.

In a strange way, she knows the story is true, the story is about her. Not the girl she is now, but perhaps the girl she used to be before they locked her in this room.

But who was that girl? A girl should remember her own name, if nothing else. Why is her brain so fuzzy?

Near the end of the picture story, men on horses gallop to the house. They must be the ones who come to her door at night. Did they draw the pictures to scare her?

There are other paintings in the room, real paintings, beautiful paintings. A few hang on the walls, but most lean against the wall. The same people are in most of them. A pretty woman, a little girl with yellow hair, a bearded man — a family. She pretends she's the little girl. The woman is her mother. The man is her father.

She must have had a mother and a father once. Doesn't everyone?

She talks to them, and she talks for them. They have long, made-up conversations that she never remembers for more than a day.

If only she could bring them to life. They look so real. Why can't they step out of the paintings and keep her company?

✦

Years pass. The girl stops looking at the drawings on the wall. She wearies of the people in the paintings. What good are they to her? They're just faces on canvas. Flat. They cannot see her or hear her. They cannot talk to her. They cannot help her. They are useless.

She turns their faces to the wall. She forgets they are there.

✦

Seasons follow each other round and round like clockwork figures. Leaves fall, snow falls, rain falls. Flowers bloom, flowers wilt, flowers die. Snow falls again. And again. And again.

Birds nest under the eaves and sometimes find their way into the room. Trees grow taller. Their branches spread. Young trees surround the house. They push against its walls. In the summer, their leaves press against the only window and block the sunlight. The room is a dim green cave.

Brambles and vines climb the stone walls. Their roots burrow into cracks and crevices, and they cling tight. Tendrils manage to find their way inside. Every year, their leaves fall on the floor of her room.

Gradually the house blends into the woods, and people forget it's there.

The girl stays in the locked room and waits. She no longer knows who or what she is waiting for. Something, someone . . .

She is lonelier than you can imagine.

2

The Girl

One morning, the girl hears loud noises from somewhere outside. It sounds as if an army has invaded
the woods, bent on attacking and destroying everything in
its path.

Confused and frightened, the girl hides in her nest.
Buried completely under the rags of dresses, she hears
sounds she can't identify, louder even than thunder. They
come closer. The trees surrounding the house crash to the
ground. Sunlight pours through the window. She squints
and shields her eyes with her hand.

Outside, near the house, men shout. Who are they?
Where have they come from? Why are they here? Have they
come for her?

She smells smoke. They must be burning something.

Suppose the fire spreads to the house? She trembles. She'll have no place to hide.

Men enter the house. They tramp about downstairs. They speak in loud voices. They come to the second floor and then the third. Their footsteps stop at her door. The doorknob turns, but without the key, the men can't come in.

The girl burrows deeper into the rags. She doesn't think they're the ones who come on horseback at night. They don't pound on the door or shout at her, but she doesn't want them to know she's here — just in case. So she remains absolutely still.

Just outside her door, she hears a man say, "This is the only room in the house that's locked. Should we bust it open and take a look?"

The girl cringes in her hiding place. She's sure the men will find her.

"Nah," says another. "Nothing in there but trash and broken stuff."

The men shuffle past the door and go downstairs, laughing about something as they go.

When she's sure they won't come back, she tiptoes to the window and looks out. A huge yellow machine with long, jointed arms lifts and lowers, lifts and lowers, scooping up things from one place and dumping them somewhere else. Its jaws have sharp teeth.

Not far from the yellow machine are red machines with scrapers attached to their fronts. They push mounds of grassy earth into piles of red clay. Other machines have rollers that flatten everything, even hills.

She's never seen anything like these contraptions. They're bigger than steam locomotives and much scarier. Trains stay on tracks; they can't hurt you if you stay off the tracks. But these machines can go anywhere. Nothing is safe from them.

While they work, the machines roar and snort and make beeping sounds. They puff clouds of smoke into the air. The girl covers her ears, but she can still hear the noise they make.

A flash of movement catches her eye. A rabbit runs across the muddy ground. She holds her breath and prays the machines won't kill him. He disappears behind a pile of tree stumps, and she lets out her breath in a long sigh.

But where will the rabbit live? The fields have been destroyed, the woods chopped down. The men and their machines are everywhere. She wishes she could go outside and bring the rabbit to her room.

✦

Day after day, the girl watches the wreckage spread. The men and their machines cut down more trees and destroy barns and sheds. They haul furniture from the house. Sofas and chairs, their velvet upholstery stained, faded, and torn. Stuffing hangs out of holes. She sees a bed missing a leg, a bureau without drawers, a large broken mirror, fancy tables with cracked marble tops.

Did she once sit on that sofa, curl up in those chairs, sleep in that bed, look at herself in that mirror? Now everything is ruined. It's of no use to her or anyone else.

The men pile up the broken furniture and set fire to it. The smoke drifts up to her window and stings her eyes. She feels as if she's watching her life turn to ashes along with the sofas and chairs.

The men don't stop with the furniture. They burn tree stumps, carts, wagons, fences, and stacks of boards. The fire smolders for days. After dark, the embers glow and the night wind teases flickers of flames from charred wood. The smell of smoke poisons the air.

When nothing's left to burn, the men turn the fields to mud and plow roads through them. On the flat land below her window, they dig deep square holes. Their nightmare machines destroy everything in their way. Her world disappears before her eyes.

Then comes a quiet time. Machines still shake the ground, but they're down on the flat land now, hard at work building houses. The girl's home is empty again. Peaceful. She spends most of her time at the window, watching and listening, enjoying the summer breeze and the smell of honeysuckle.

She keeps her eyes focused on the distant mountains, blue and serene against the sky. She doesn't look at the fields and meadows destroyed by the machines.

One afternoon she dreams of a picnic by a stream. She's sitting under a tree with a man and a woman. She's had this dream many times. But it always ends before she's ready. She wakes up reaching for the man and woman, but it's too late. They're gone, and she's alone in the locked room.

3

Jules

It was August, hot and humid. The air conditioner in the truck wasn't working. My T-shirt stuck to my back, and Mom's hair had changed from smooth and sleek in the morning to frizzy and curly in the afternoon. The three of us sat elbow to elbow in the front bench seat, Dad driving, Mom beside him, and me next to the open window.

After spending most of the day on the Interstate, we were now on a narrow country road that twisted and turned, uphill and down, passing house trailers tucked away in the woods, tumbledown barns in weedy fields, cows grazing in pastures, and farmhouses at the end of long lanes.

I'd gotten tired of asking if we were almost there, so I closed my eyes and concentrated on not getting carsick. The bumping and swaying were definitely affecting my stomach. Why had I drunk that disgusting milk shake?

At last Dad said, "We're here."

I opened my eyes and saw a sign welcoming us to Oak Hill — "A future community of luxury homes designed and built by Stonybrook."

Ahead of us, a bumpy dirt road looped around the foundations of future luxury homes. On top of a hill above the construction site stood an old stone house. The land around it had been scraped down to raw red clay, rutted with tire tracks filled with muddy water. Waist-high weeds had sprung up everywhere. Piles of uprooted stumps, tree trunks, branches, and rocks waited to be hauled away.

I stared at the old house in dismay. Three stories tall and built of stone, it loomed above us, dark and empty against a cloudy sky. Sheets of weathered plywood hid its windows. A blue plastic tarp covered the roof. Its edges lifted when the wind blew, making an eerie flapping sound.

Dad specialized in restoring historic houses like this one, so for as long as I could remember, we'd lived like nomads, moving from place to place, staying in each one long enough for him to complete the job. Some of them had been scary. Their steps creaked at night, footsteps crossed their floors, their doors opened and shut without cause, but not one of them had been as frightening as Oak Hill.

Even from a distance, I knew something bad had happened in that house. Maybe it was the crows perched in a line on the roof, maybe it was the utter desolation of the scene, but the word *foreboding* came to mind, along with *haunted, misery, and sorrow.* It was the perfect setting for a ghost story.

"You weren't exaggerating," Mom said to Dad. "The house is practically in ruins. Are you sure it's worth fixing up?"

"Stonybrook has big plans for it," Dad said. "When the restoration's done, the house will be an inn. I'm told it's to be the jewel in the crown of the Oak Hill community. The perfect place for guests and potential buyers to stay."

I looked at Dad. "Please tell me we are not *living* in that house."

Dad laughed. "Of course not, Jules. The corporation built an addition on the back of the house for us. Modern kitchen, family room, two bedrooms, two bathrooms. New heating system, air conditioning, Internet, satellite TV — all the necessities."

"Oh, Ron," Mom said. "I thought we were staying in Oak Hill. I've always wanted to live in a haunted house."

I didn't know whether she was serious or joking. With Mom, it was hard to tell, but if she meant what she'd said,

I had even more reason to be scared. I shuddered. "Do you really think it's haunted?" I asked her.

"No, of course not." She laughed. "I was just being silly."

"Ha-hah, some joke," I said, only slightly relieved.

Dad patted my shoulder as we got out of the truck. "Don't worry, Jules. The only thing wrong with Oak Hill is dry rot, termite damage, leaks in the roof, mold, and mildew—the plagues of every old building I've ever worked on. No ghosts, I promise."

I felt a little better, but not much. It would take more than Dad's promise to convince me the house wasn't haunted.

"Can we go inside?" Mom asked.

Dad smiled. "I'll give you the grand tour."

Mom and I followed him up the sagging front steps, she eagerly, I reluctantly. Dad pulled an old-fashioned iron key from his pocket and struggled to unlock the door.

"Maybe it's the wrong key," I said, hoping the door wouldn't open.

Ignoring me, Dad continued to jiggle the key. After some pushing, pulling, and a little swearing, he finally got the door open. "Keys like this are works of art," he said, "but not easy to use."

The darkness inside the house exhaled dampness, old

cellars, and decay, but Dad ushered us inside as if he were leading us into a king's palace. "Try to picture this place as it was a couple of hundred years ago," he said. "Polished floors. a curving staircase, sunlight falling through tall windows. I can't wait to bring it back to life, to reveal its beauty."

While Dad raved, I stopped on the threshold, overwhelmed by a sense that something hid in the shadows, listening, watching, waiting. I'd often had feelings like this, but nothing had ever come of them. I'd seen no ghosts, and as the days passed, I'd stopped looking for them. This time, my fear was more intense than usual.

"What's wrong, Jules?" Mom looked at me with concern. "Is your stomach still upset?"

"I'm kind of queasy from that strawberry milk shake." I made a face. "Maybe some fresh air . . ." I backed out of the doorway, into the warmth of the sun.

Mom seized my hand and stopped me. "We'll just take a quick look. Then you can lie down for a while before dinner."

"Come on, Jules," Dad said. "This house is magnificent. I want you to see it as it is now so you can appreciate my work when I'm finished. It's probably the best project I've ever had."

Light from the open door illuminated crumbling walls

streaked with stains and mold. In one corner a huge wasp nest clung to the ceiling. Bird poop splattered the floor, along with a scattering of feathers, tiny bones, and dead insects. A heavy tree limb had crashed through the roof and landed on the steps to the second floor. Its branches had smashed the banister, and the entire staircase tilted to one side.

"Just look at those marble fireplaces," Mom said. "Can't you picture velvet drapes, crystal chandeliers, polished tables, carpets, paintings on the walls. . . . I can just imagine the people who lived here, women in long dresses, bearded gentlemen."

"Maybe you could use the house as a setting for your next book," Dad said.

"What a great idea. I've always wanted to write a historical novel. Maybe a ghost story or a gothic mystery." Her voice trailed off, as if she were thinking about the possibilities.

"You need to finish the one you're working on now," Dad reminded her.

Mom sighed. "I'm so tired of coming up with new mysteries for Inspector Turner to solve."

She took a step, and the floor groaned under her feet.

"Careful." Dad rocked on his heels and bounced. The boards creaked under his weight but held firm. "The floor's fairly solid here, but it's caved in elsewhere." He glanced at me. "It's strictly off-limits to you, Jules. Don't get any ideas about exploring."

I looked at Dad in wonder. Did he actually think I'd set foot in this terrifying place by myself?

"How old is Oak Hill?" Mom asked.

"When I looked at the property last month, I visited the county courthouse and did some research—land records, wills, census returns," Dad said. "I like to get a feeling for a house—when it was built, who lived there, that sort of thing. A man named Pettifer built Oak Hill in 1786."

"When was it abandoned?" I asked.

"Sometime after the 1880 census was taken," Dad said. "Henry Bennett and his family lived here then. That's the last reference I found."

"Where did they go?" I asked. "What happened to them?"

"I doubt anyone living today could answer that question."

Mom sneezed three times in a row. "The dust and mildew are getting to me," she said. "Let's go see our living quarters."

Dad led us into a room that once must have been a kitchen. A stained and rusty sink lay on the floor as if it had simply fallen off the wall. Rusty pots and pans had been swept into a corner along with broken china and odds and ends of rubble. Vines crept through cracks in the plywood covering the windows. The bones of a small animal lay in another corner.

Unlocking a new door with a modern key, Dad ushered us into a sunny kitchen. A sliding glass door led to a deck overlooking a field and the woods beyond. Light spilled from skylights in the family room ceiling. In one corner was a big fireplace made of stone.

"Oh, Ron," Mom said, "it's beautiful. I love it!"

It was definitely better than the old house, but it shared a wall with it—which meant it was too close to those dark, empty rooms for me. Sometimes we lived in an apartment in town while Dad worked on a house. I liked that arrangement better.

Our furniture was already in place, moved here by Stonybrook. All we had to do was unload the truck and bring in our suitcases and boxes of personal things that Mom hadn't trusted to a moving company.

My bedroom was across the hall from Mom and Dad's. Light poured through a floor-to-ceiling window and a skylight, something I'd wanted all my life. I moved one of my twin beds under it so I could look up at the stars and the moon before I fell asleep.

Thanks to Dad's job, we'd moved in and out of many houses, so I was a pro when it came to organizing my things. In less than an hour, I'd put my clothes away, unpacked my books, and charged my iPad.

Last of all, I made my bed and lay down, tired from the long drive from Ohio to Virginia.

From where I lay, I could see the back of the old house from my window. My eyes moved from one boarded-up window to the next, first floor to second floor to third floor, where the windows were smaller.

Oddly, one window hadn't been boarded up. Its small panes caught the afternoon light.

Something moved behind the glass but disappeared so quickly, I wasn't sure what I'd seen. I blinked and looked again. Nothing moved.

I told myself it must have been a trick of the light, a reflection, my imagination, but I wasn't convinced. I'd seen something at that window, just as I'd sensed something listening when Dad showed us the house. We weren't alone in Oak Hill.

Suddenly I didn't want to be alone in my room, scaring

myself with silly thoughts. Turning my back on the house and its secrets, I went looking for Mom and Dad.

Mom was in the kitchen, putting the finishing touches on a salad, and Dad was carving the roasted chicken we'd bought before we turned off the highway.

"You're just in time," Dad said. "We're having dinner outside on the deck." He gestured at the sliding glass doors, open to the fresh evening air. "Our first meal at Oak Hill."

"Maybe tomorrow we'll find a good place for a picnic," Mom said. "What do you two think?"

"Definitely a picnic," I said, "in a meadow by a stream."

"A meadow by a stream." Dad smiled. "How do you know we'll find a place like that?"

I shrugged. "It just popped into my head."

While we ate, I pictured us sitting under a willow tree, listening to water running over pebbles and stones. We'd watch minnows and those funny long-legged water bugs. Gerridae, my sixth-grade science teacher called them. I saw the scene so vividly it seemed like a memory of something I'd done.

"Well, what do you think of our accommodations, Jules?" Dad asked. "A lot better than that dingy apartment in Cleveland, right?"

"Not to mention the Chicago third-floor walkup," said Mom, "or the house with the leaky roof in Indiana."

"It's nice," I said, "but if you want to know the truth, I'd rather live in town."

"What do you mean, honey? This is a great place," Dad said. "And it's provided at no cost by the corporation. We don't often get free housing."

Mom waved her arm at the woods behind the house. Tall trees hid the shopping centers strung along the highway and muffled the traffic's roar. "Just look at that view. Why on earth would you want to live in town?"

"In town, there's stuff to do—a swimming pool, a library, movie theaters, kids my age. I'll never make any friends out here. When school starts, I won't know a single soul!"

"It's only a fifteen-minute drive into Hillsborough," Mom said. "We can go anytime you want."

"But that's not all. Oak Hill is right outside my bedroom window. It's ugly and dark and scary, and I hate it."

Dad leaned across the table and patted my hand. "It's only temporary, Jules. In another year or so, we'll be living somewhere else."

"But Dad, that's just the point. I've told you over and

over again how sick I am of changing schools and losing friends and getting behind on stuff. It's not fair, Dad. I want to live like ordinary people, not like some kind of nomad." I glared at him. It was the angriest I'd ever been with him. "This house is just the last straw!"

Dad started to say something, but I wasn't finished. "Cleveland, St. Louis, Detroit, Chicago, Philadelphia, St. Paul, Baltimore—" I said. "They all run together in my head. I can't remember how many houses we've lived in or all the schools I've gone to."

I fought to keep myself from crying. Why couldn't they understand what it was like for me? Always the new girl, always trying to fit in, wearing the wrong clothes, making friends just to leave them behind and start all over again somewhere else.

Mom looked at Dad. "Maybe we should think about what Jules is saying. She's almost thirteen, Ron. It's hard for her to change schools every year. She needs to settle down and make friends."

Dad sighed and took a few swallows of iced tea. "When I was your age, Jules, I couldn't wait to grow up and get out of Plainsville. The day I left for college . . ."

Long before Dad stopped talking, I stopped listening. I'd heard it all before. His boring hometown, his father's boring job running a furniture store, his mother's boring bridge club, his aunts and his uncles, his neighbors, all stuck in the same boring routines year after year. Most of them had never been more than a hundred miles from home. In their eyes, Plainsville had everything any human being needed. The outside world was a dangerous place.

That life hadn't been for Dad. He'd seen most of the world by the time he was twenty-five. You'd think by now he'd be ready to settle down, but oh, no, he was still on the road.

Mom interrupted him. "But Ron, couldn't you at least consider—"

"I go where the work is, you know that." He poured himself another glass of iced tea. "Restoring old buildings is my passion. When I have a chance to renovate a grand house like this one, how can I say no?"

Too annoyed to say another word, I watched the moon rise over the darkening field. The clouds had blown away, and a nearly full moon hung just above the treetops. The sky was studded with stars, more than I'd ever seen.

I pictured the mysterious Bennett family looking at the same stars and the same moon. They'd heard the chorus of cicadas in the trees, they'd seen the flash of lightning bugs in the woods, they'd felt the evening breeze cool their skin. Just like I did now.

I imagined the Bennetts strolling across the field—a man, a woman, and maybe a daughter, a family like mine, enjoying a summer night. They seemed to step from my imagination into the real world. The man said something, and the little girl laughed. I stared at them, entranced, convinced now that they were real people, out for an evening walk.

Just as I was about to beckon them to join us, Dad yawned loudly. The family immediately disappeared into the woods.

Perplexed, I turned to Mom. "Did you see those people?"

"Where?" She peered at the field. "I don't see anyone out there."

"They're gone now, but they were just there." I pointed to the spot. "A man, a woman, and a little girl."

Dad shook his head. "No one lives within miles of this place, Jules."

"But I'm sure—"

"Your eyes were tricked by shadows," Mom said. "You saw a bush, a small tree, that's all."

Maybe that was it. I was tired, and it was hard to focus without much light. But still—they seemed real when I saw them. And I'd heard the girl laugh.

I looked again at the edge of the field. The family must

have taken a path into the woods. If they'd really been there, that is. Dad was right. No one lived near Oak Hill. Where had they come from? Like Mom said, my eyes must have been tricked by the darkness.

Dad swatted a mosquito. "It's a long drive from Ohio to Virginia." He yawned again. "I don't know about you two, but I'm ready for bed."

Mom gathered up the paper plates and cups, and Dad and I helped her carry everything inside. We dumped the remains of dinner into the trash. No dishes to wash tonight.

Dad yawned again. "The crew arrives at eight a.m. tomorrow to start work," Dad reminded us. "Better be up, dressed, and ready."

Mom groaned and followed him into their bedroom.

Too tired even to open a book, I undressed quickly, fell into bed, closed my eyes, and went to sleep.

Long before daylight, a loud noise woke me. Thunder, I thought at first, but no, that wasn't it. As the noise grew louder, I realized it was the sound of horses galloping toward the house. On they came, two or three of them, running fast and hard though the dark. A man shouted in anger, a woman called out in fear.

Frightened, I sat up and peered out my window. The moon threw shadows everywhere, slicing the night into a confusing pattern of blacks and whites. I saw no horses, no riders. I heard nothing but the wind in the trees and the *bang bang bang* of a loose shutter striking the side of the old house. If horses and riders had come this way, the darkness had swallowed them up.

I slid under the covers and shivered, not just from the cool night air but also from fear. What was going on? I hadn't been at Oak Hill for twenty-four hours, and I'd already seen something move at a window on the third floor, watched a family crossing a field at twilight, and heard the steady beat of horses' hooves pounding toward the old house.

The night was silent now. Nothing moved. Yet a presence lingered in the stillness. I wanted to run across the hall to my parents' room and tell them what I'd seen, but I knew they'd say I was dreaming.

Maybe they were right. Maybe not. Either way, they'd be annoyed if I woke them up in the middle of the night.

Maybe tomorrow I'd talk to Mom and Dad. Maybe they'd heard the horses too. Maybe they'd believe me. . . . Maybe they wouldn't.

Finally, too exhausted to worry about what Mom and Dad would or would not believe, I curled up like a child, shut my eyes, and fell asleep.

4

The Girl

The girl stands at the window and peers down at the addition. A light goes on. She draws back, frightened. The light isn't soft, like the glow from a candle or a kerosene lamp, but harsh and more brilliant than any she's ever seen.

A girl, a big girl, walks past the window. She has long dark hair, and she's tall.

Once, she thinks, long ago, she might have had friends like that dark-haired girl. She can't recall their faces or names or what they said, but she thinks that sometimes they laughed together. It's been a long time since she's had anything to laugh about.

Maybe they were never real, those friends. It's hard to be sure of anything except this room and what she sees from the window.

But the dark-haired girl in the addition is definitely real. She watches her move around her room, then change her clothes and get into bed.

Once, the girl in the locked room must have slept, but not now. She's tired all the time, but never sleepy. Just sad and scared and lonely.

The light in the room goes out; the girl is alone again.

She watches the dark-haired girl's window long after the light goes out. The moonlight is bright on the wall of the addition, but it casts dark shadows on the grass beneath her window.

Suddenly she steps back into the shadows. Now is the time of night when they come, she thinks, and sure enough, no sooner has she thought it than she hears the horses. Their hooves pound the earth. A man yells. A woman cries out in fear.

She senses that the dark-haired girl is awake and frightened. She wishes she could tell her that the men are not after her. It is the girl in the locked room the men want.

They're at the kitchen door now. Soon they'll come upstairs. She scurries to the wardrobe and hides in her nest.

While the men shout, while the woman waits in the yard, she comforts herself by thinking about the dark-haired girl. Perhaps she'll see her in the morning. She'll watch her and learn about her. Perhaps the girl is the one she waits for. Perhaps she will rescue her. Perhaps she will free her from this room.

5

Jules

The foreman of Dad's crew and two of his assistants arrived just after breakfast. They spread out plans on the kitchen table and began talking about the morning's work.

Dad looked at Mom. "Why don't you and Jules go for a walk? Maybe you'll find that stream and we'll have a picnic there."

Mom turned to me with a smile, and we left Dad to pore over his plans with his crew.

Not sure where we wanted to go, we wandered across a field and found a narrow path that led downhill through a field of wildflowers.

At the bottom of the hill, Mom stopped. "Listen. I hear water running, a creek or a stream. Let's find it."

We ran through the weeds and ducked under the

branches of a willow tree. A shallow stream, almost wide enough to be a river, ran past.

Mom kicked off her sandals and splashed into the water near the bank. The water was so clear I could have counted the stones on the sandy bottom.

Mom held her hand out to me. "Come on, Jules. The water's a little cold, but it's only ankle-deep here."

When I hesitated, she laughed and kicked water at me.

"Stop it." I drew back. "Come out of there."

"Look." She pointed at a school of minnows swimming past. "And water striders."

"Their official name is Gerridae," I told her.

"Where on earth did you learn that?"

"Last year, from my sixth-grade science teacher."

Mom laughed. "Well, I'm going to call them water striders. It suits them better." She leaned over and watched the insects move across the stream's smooth surface. "Gerridae indeed."

Suddenly she grabbed my hands and pulled me into the water.

"Mom!" I shouted. "I still have my shoes on!"

"They're rubber flip-flops. It won't hurt them to get wet, and it won't hurt you either."

"The stones are slippery. I'm going to fall."

"Goodness, Jules, don't be such a scaredy-cat." Mom took my hand and led me deeper into the water. It wasn't as bad as I'd feared. Sunlight splashed down through the willow leaves. Minnows darted around us, their silver bellies flashing as they turned, and the Gerridae walked in circles on the still water near the shore. If I slipped and fell, I'd get wet, but I wouldn't drown. The day was so hot, it might even feel nice.

Mom smiled. "It's fun, right?"

I laughed and splashed her. She splashed me. I splashed back. By the time we hauled ourselves out of the stream, our jeans were soaked to our hips and we were laughing so hard we could hardly walk.

"Let's bring Dad next time," Mom said. "It's the perfect spot for a picnic."

It was perfect, almost too perfect. I'd imagined a place like this, and here it was—exactly as I'd pictured it. The stream, the willow tree, the field. I felt as if I'd waded in the stream before, watched the Gerridae and the minnows, seen the sun shine through the willow's leaves. When a rabbit hopped into sight, I knew he'd disappear into a thicket of honeysuckle.

I'd had this feeling often. I'd ride my bike past a house and think I'd seen it before, even though I'd never been on that road. Sometimes I'd be talking to someone and know what she'd say next.

I asked Mom about it once, and she told me the experience is called *déjà vu*—French for *already seen*. She had it too; almost everyone did.

But this time the sensation was strong enough to make me uneasy. Turning to Mom, I asked, "Does this place seem familiar to you?"

She looked around, taking in the willow tree, the stream, the fields rolling away toward the mountains. "It reminds me of a park in Ohio where we picnicked. The field, the stream, the trees—very similar. No mountains, though." She laughed. "It was definitely a different place. We've never been here before."

I looked around and shook my head. "I don't remember any picnics in Ohio."

"Well, you were only two or three years old, too little to remember, but it's probably imprinted in your memory."

Mom flopped down on her back and patted the ground beside her. "Let's lie here for a while and let the sun dry our clothes."

I lay down and watched clouds float across the sky like a flock of sheep wandering across a wide blue field. Birds sang, leaves blew in the breeze. I let my mind drift with the clouds.

While I lay there, I had a strange feeling that someone had joined Mom and me. Turning my head, I saw a little girl sitting near me, her face hidden by long yellow hair. She wore an old-fashioned dress, and a doll with a china head lay beside her. The girl was weaving a chain of clover blossoms, her fingers quick and deft as she tied the stems together. She sang too softly for me to hear the words, but the tune was familiar.

Suddenly she turned her head and looked at me. She opened her mouth as if to speak, but a woman called, "Come along, darling. It's time to go home."

The girl turned toward her mother, held up the clover chain, and laughed. "Look what I've made for you, Mama! A crown!"

Before I had a chance to ask who she was, the girl vanished, just like that. She was here, and then she wasn't.

I jumped up to see where she'd gone. I saw no tree close enough for her to hide behind. Not a ripple in the grass betrayed her hiding place.

"Where are you?" I called. "Come back."

Mom opened her eyes and sat up. "Who are you talking to, Jules?" She looked around at the empty field. "Is someone here?"

"A girl was sitting right there." I pointed to the spot a

few feet away from me. "She was making a clover chain. I thought she was about to tell me something, but her mother called her and she disappeared."

Mom shook her head. "You must have been dreaming, Jules."

"She was *right there!*" I pointed again, just in case Mom had looked for the girl in the wrong place.

"Where is she now?" Mom asked. "People don't just disappear into thin air."

"I know, I know, but Mom, listen to me. I *saw* her. I even heard her tell her mother she made the clover chain for her." I stared at the place where the girl had sat. I hadn't been sleeping, I hadn't been dreaming; she'd been there and I'd seen her.

Mom held my face close to hers and stared into my eyes. "Jules, you've always had vivid dreams," Mom said. "I remember one particularly, a nightmare. You claimed it really happened."

"What are you talking about?"

Mom leaned back on her hands and smiled. "You must have been four or five. We were living in Vermont at the time—your father had been hired to turn a barn into a house and studio for an artist, and we were staying in an old farmhouse on the property. Almost every single night you'd climb into bed with Dad and me, crying, shivering, scared. There was an old woman in your room, you'd claim, sitting in the rocking chair by your bed. The moon shone through the window and lit her white hair but hid her face in shadows. She was knitting a sweater.

"You heard her needles click and clack. You heard the chair creak. 'As soon as this sweater is finished,' she told you, 'I'm going to put it on you and take you away with me.' 'No,' you'd cry, 'no.' She'd cackle, and you'd jump out of bed and run to our room, crying and screaming."

I stared at Mom. "I don't remember that."

Mom laughed. "Well, I do. You woke us up night after night. The sweater was getting bigger, you said. Soon it would fit you, and she'd take you away. We told you it was a dream, but you said she was a real live witch. Your dad and I took you to your room and showed you the empty rocking chair, but you said she was in the corner, hiding in the shadows, or under your bed, or in the closet. We turned on the lights. No one was there. But you still insisted she was real."

While Mom talked, the image of an old woman popped into my head. She sat by my bed knitting a sweater. The moon lit her hair, but not her face. Every night the sweater was bigger.

"Aha," Mom said, "you *do* remember!"

I nodded slowly. "She was going to take me away. I'd never see you again. I was so scared."

"But now," Mom said, "you know the old woman was a dream. She wasn't real—just like the girl in the field."

No, I thought, *not* like the girl in the field. When I saw the girl, I was wide-awake, and I wasn't scared.

"You were a fearful child with a big imagination," Mom went on. "It's no wonder you had bad dreams."

I didn't want to spoil the day arguing with Mom, but no matter what she said, the girl hadn't been a dream. Certainly not a bad dream.

"Perhaps it's the house," Mom mused. "I know it scares you. Maybe it unsettles your mind—the people you saw last night, the girl today. Maybe they're manifestations of your anxiety."

I ignored Mom. She loved probing her characters' fictional minds to uncover their motives for doing things. Well, I was real, not fictional, and I didn't like her attempts to analyze me.

While she talked, I watched a summer breeze race across the field, rippling the weeds. Trees bent to and fro. Leaves sighed and rustled. For a moment I glimpsed the flutter of a white dress in the woods, but it was gone too quickly for me to be sure it was the girl.

Mom got to her feet. "Let's go home. It must be lunchtime."

I walked behind her, dragging my feet, unsure what to believe. Mom was right about one thing — the girl had vanished too quickly to be real.

What if the people I'd seen were ghosts? The thought stopped me in the middle of the path. I'd come to the edge of the woods, and I shivered in the shade.

But how could that be true? Ghosts don't appear in the daytime. They come at night, moaning and wailing, maybe even rattling chains. They might walk across a field at dusk, but they don't sit in a sunny field making clover chains. At least not in the stories I'd read.

Ghosts are transparent, you can see through them, they can walk through walls, but both the family and the girl were so solid, I'd thought they were real people.

I folded my arms tightly across my chest and shivered again. I hadn't been scared when I saw the girl, but I was scared now. I'd read enough ghost stories to know that the dead sometimes linger to seek help from the living or atone for a crime.

She'd seemed like an ordinary little girl, but she'd

probably been dead for a long time—which meant she was far from ordinary, and possibly dangerous.

But no. I'd looked into her face and seen nothing to fear. Surely she'd committed no crime. That left help—is help what she wanted from me? How was I to help a ghost?

6

The Girl

The girl is at the window again. Earlier, she'd watched the dark-haired girl and her mother walk down a path that led away from the house. She'd heard them laughing and talking, but soon the trees swallowed them up and they were gone.

She thinks they went to a field where a willow grows. If she closes her eyes, she sees the dark-haired girl sitting in the grass, but it must be a dream. She hasn't left this room, not once in — oh, ever so much time, oceans of time. But her dream is so vivid. She's sitting in the grass near the girl. She's making something. A clover chain. Yes, that's what it is. She remembers the limp stems and the fading blossoms and the way she knotted them together.

But who is the chain for? Not the dark-haired girl or her mother, who is fast asleep. It's for someone else.

The dark-haired girl looks at her. That girl is about to speak when someone calls her. The dream ends, and the girl is at the window again.

She sighs. Even though it was a dream, she feels as if she really left the room and sat outside in the sunlight. She remembers its warmth and the sound of bees buzzing in the clover. She'd like to visit the field again and see the other girl. Maybe this time the dream will last longer. She thinks she needs to tell that girl something. If only she could remember what it is — or why she should tell her.

Now she waits for the girl and her mother to return. She's not sure how long they've been gone. Hours, days, and years blend together in the most confusing way, a flow of light and dark, light and dark.

When the sun is high above the house, she hears them coming. Mother first, the dark-haired girl following behind. The girl is very quiet. She looks worried. She doesn't look up at the window. Her head down, she follows her mother into the addition.

Below her, out of sight, a door opens and closes. Once more, the girl in the locked room is alone at her window.

7

Jules

After lunch, Mom opened her laptop and got to work on book four of a mystery series set in Maine. I knew better than to interrupt her when she was writing.

I grabbed a book and sat outside in the shade cast by the picnic table's big green umbrella. In the old house, the crew ripped plywood off windows and tore up floorboards. Drills, hammers, saws—the noise made it hard to concentrate on reading.

I laid the book aside and decided to take a walk. Maybe I'd go back to the stream and sit in the shade of the willow tree. It was cooler there. And a lot quieter.

I hadn't gotten out of sight of the house when I noticed a broken wood chair poking up from the weeds. Looking closer, I saw a few window frames and a heap of warped boards. The cleanup crew must have forgotten to haul the stuff away. Maybe they hadn't even seen it.

In one of my history classes, I'd learned about middens, the name for places where people threw their trash in olden days. Archaeologists discover a lot about the past from what they find in middens, our teacher said.

Suppose I'd found the place where the Bennetts threw their trash?

I squatted down and poked in the weeds. This would be my dig. If I dug deep enough, I'd unearth older, more interesting stuff, things the Bennetts had owned. Like an archaeologist, I'd learn about the family from what they'd thrown away.

I found a large bent spoon and used it to dig in the muddy ground. At first, all I found were broken china, misshapen forks and spoons, fragments of wood, scraps of cloth—odds and ends that told me nothing about the Bennetts or what had happened to them.

With a sigh, I turned back to the midden. I was hot and sweaty now, and a cloud of gnats had discovered me. Just as I was about to quit, I saw a small hand sticking out of the muddy ground. I drew back, startled, but almost immediately realized it was the hand not of a baby, but of a doll.

Carefully I dug around it and eased it gently out of the ground. The doll's hollow china head was bald, she had no eyes, and her face was cracked and chipped. Her leather body was stained, and her arms and legs dangled loosely from it. One hand was missing altogether, and the other had no fingers.

Although the doll looked more like a dead body than a toy, I laid her carefully on the grass with the other broken things. Perhaps she belonged to the girl I'd seen in the field. She'd had a doll with her. It had been beautiful, not hideous, but the doll from the midden might have looked like that once.

I studied the doll's damaged face. Yes — with eyes that opened and shut, rosy cheeks, a wig of long curls, and a pretty dress, she'd look just like the one lying beside the girl. Maybe Mom would know of a place that repaired antique dolls.

Turning back to my dig, I probed the earth gently, the way I thought an archaeologist would, hoping to discover other things the girl once owned. I dug up a noseless china shepherd, an armless shepherdess, and several tailless dogs, most of them lacking a leg or two as well.

My favorite discovery was a set of seven small china

dolls. The two largest were about five inches tall, but the others were much smaller, just two or three inches. Each was molded in one piece, so neither their arms nor their legs moved. Their hair was painted on, and their painted faces were almost worn away.

I laid them beside the ugly bald doll and lined them up from biggest to smallest. I pictured the girl playing with them in a dollhouse built by her father. I saw her kneeling on the floor, her hair hiding her face, and moving the dolls on their tiny feet from room to room, *click click click*.

Then I heard a tiny, scratchy voice begin to speak. *"I'm scared,"* the littlest doll said.

"Hush," said the biggest one. *"Go upstairs and lock yourself in your room before the bad men get you."*

Frightened, I dropped the dolls and spun around to see who'd spoken. No one was behind me, but when I looked up at the window on the third floor, I saw something that might have been a small figure almost hidden in shadows.

I jumped to my feet. "Who said that? Where are you?"

Whoever had been at the window was gone. At my feet, the little dolls lay silently in the weeds where I'd dropped them. Beside them was an old key, about six inches long, coated with rust and mud. How had I missed seeing it?

I picked the key up and examined its scrollwork and fancy details. It weighed heavy in my hand—a serious key, an important key, a powerful key. A key to what?

The sun was lower now, and the long shadow of the house lay like a dark hand over the midden and the things I'd found. Suddenly I didn't want any of them—the bent silverware or the broken china, the ugly bald doll or the little china figurines. They were the possessions of dead people, contaminated somehow. I dumped them into the hole I'd dug and shoved dirt on top. This time, they'd stay buried.

Without looking at the third floor, I walked away quickly, but I couldn't escape the sensation of being watched. The little girl was in that room. I was convinced of it.

Was she afraid of me? Was I afraid of her? Should she be? Should I be?

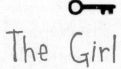

8

The Girl

The girl in the locked room looks down from her window and sees the dark-haired girl from the addition digging in the kitchen midden, of all places. It's the first time she's gotten a good look at her. If it weren't for her long hair, the girl would mistake her for a boy. She's wearing short pants. Her shirt is shapeless. Something the girl can't read is written on its front. Her feet are bare. And dirty.

She doesn't know what to make of the girl's appearance.

Not even the poorest of girls wears clothes like that. And children don't go barefoot unless they cannot afford shoes.

Everything in the midden is trash, yet the dark-haired girl has picked bits of porcelain, medicine bottles, tarnished silver, and broken dishes from the rubbish as if they were valuable. She's even dug up a broken doll, which seems vaguely familiar.

Perhaps the doll once belonged to her. Yes, it must have. But surely it was prettier then, not broken and bald as it is now. It distresses her to look at the doll. She turns away.

Later she returns to the window. The dark-haired girl is still there. If she expects to find treasure buried along with the trash, she'll be sorely disappointed. Indeed, she already looks disappointed. She swats at gnats, she pushes her hair out of her face, she's hot and impatient.

But she keeps digging. She finds a group of tiny dolls and lays them beside the ugly doll.

The girl's fingers remember how those dolls feel, cool and smooth and hard. They're dirty and chipped now, but she remembers making them talk. What should they say now?

Perhaps the littlest one says, *"I'm scared."*

And the big one says, *"Hush. Go upstairs and lock yourself in your room before the bad men get you."*

Suddenly the dark-haired girl drops the dolls and looks around. Something seems to have frightened her. Did she hear what the dolls said?

Fearful of being seen, the girl in the locked room ducks below the window but slowly raises her head to see what the dark-haired girl does next.

She's throwing all the things she found into the hole she dug. Even the little dolls. She's finally realized it's trash, nothing but trash.

Then the dark-haired girl looks down and sees a key. She picks it up and turns it slowly, as if she's examining it.

The girl crosses her fingers and whispers, "Don't throw it away. Keep it. Find the lock it fits."

The dark-haired girl can't possibly know which lock the key fits, but what if she tries the key in every door? She'll come closer and closer—from the first floor to the second, from the second floor to the third. She can almost hear the girl's footsteps, rather like a story she heard once long ago about a teeny-tiny woman who stole a teeny-tiny bone. . . .

She imagines the girl stopping at her door and poking the key into the lock. She'll jiggle it back and forth, take it out, and poke it in again. *Jiggle, jiggle, jiggle.* Finally, the door will open and the dark-haired girl will enter the room. It will be the first time someone has come through that door since the girl was locked in.

Everything will change. She doesn't know how she knows this. Nor does she know how things will change. Maybe for good, maybe for bad.

But how can anything be worse than it already is?

She paces around the room. Her feet leave no tracks

in the dust. Perhaps she's waited here long enough. Perhaps no one will come for her except the men. Night after night, they'll come, and she'll hide in the wardrobe. Day after day she'll stand at the window and watch the seasons change. Years will pass. Centuries. And nothing will change. Is this what she wants?

The girl tiptoes to the window. Taking care to hide in the shadows, she whispers, "Keep the key. Find the right door. Find me. Let me out."

Below her, almost as if she doesn't notice what she's doing, the girl from the addition drops the key into her pocket and walks out of sight.

The girl in the locked room claps her hands soundlessly. Soon the door will open and she will be free.

Free to do what?

"Oh, mercy," she whispers. She has no idea what she'll do when she's free.

9

Jules

Mom was where I'd left her, working on her novel. Without even looking at me, she said, "Not now, Jules, I'm busy."

I had nothing to do, nowhere to go. So I went to my room and opened my iPad. Using a drawing app, I made silly sketches of cats and dogs and horses. They weren't very good, so I deleted them, then checked my e-mail. As usual, I had no messages.

My thoughts wandered to the girl in the field. Out of curiosity, I typed in "1880 U.S. census" and hit Search. Maybe I'd spot something Dad had missed.

Most of the websites charged for accessing the census, but I finally found a free one. I entered "Bennett" for the surname as well as "married" for status and "Virginia" for residence. One hundred and fourteen Bennetts came up.

Dad had mentioned a first name. What was it?

Harry came to mind. No one with that name turned up, but the search engine coughed up several Harriet Bennetts, one Harold Bennett, and three Henry Bennetts.

Henry sounded possible, so I looked at all three Henrys. The most likely choice was thirty-two years old. His occupation was "artist." His wife was named Laura, and their daughter, Lily, was one year old.

Also in the household was a tenant farmer, his wife, and a hired man. Sure that they were of no importance, I ignored them.

I stared at my iPad, almost as mystified as before. The girl in the field must have been Lily Bennett, but I still had no idea what happened to her or why I'd seen her — or what she wanted.

I went to my window and squinted at the window on the third floor. The sun lit the glass so brightly I could see nothing behind it.

"Lily," I whispered. "Lily, tell me what to do."

No one answered. No face appeared at the window. But she was there, I knew she was.

I wished I had someone to talk to, someone who'd believe me.

"Jules," Mom called from the kitchen, "please set the table."

As I arranged plates, glasses, and cutlery, I felt a weight in my pocket and pulled out the key. I was sure I'd reburied it with the other stuff, but here it was. I'd dropped it into my pocket without noticing.

For a moment I stood still and studied the old key. "What door do you unlock?"

The answer came like a whisper of air. *Lily's door. Of course.*

Dropping the key into my pocket, I finished setting the table. My mind spun with ideas. I'd go to the third floor, I'd unlock the door, I'd free Lily. But I couldn't go there in the daylight. I'd have to wait until late at night when Dad and Mom were asleep. Was I brave enough to do that? Just thinking about it made my hands shake so badly I dropped a spoon on the floor.

I said little during dinner, but Mom and Dad were too interested in their own conversation to notice. Dad described the progress he'd made with the walls and ceiling. Mom told him about her idea to add a character to her novel—a child whose recurrent nightmares hold clues to the mystery.

"I wonder where you got that idea," I muttered, but kept my voice too low for her or Dad to hear me.

That night, I hid the key in a little wooden box where I kept special things — seashells from a Rhode Island beach, stones from a creek in Ohio, a tiny silver bracelet Grandmother had given me when I was born, a plastic palm tree pin from Florida, a broken whistle, a couple of marbles, childhood treasures worthless to everyone but me.

Before I got into bed, I looked up at the third-story window. Its glass reflected the moon, but no one stood in the darkness, staring down at me.

"Lily, Lily," I whispered, "what do you want? Why are you here?"

✦

For the next two days, it rained, a cold, hard rain. Mom and I were trapped inside, with no escape from the pounding of hammers, the whine of drills, and the roaring of power saws. Heavy feet tramped around in the old house. Men shouted over the noise of their tools. They laughed and swore.

I finished my book. With nothing else to read, I played some games on my iPad, stared out the kitchen door at the rain puddling on the deck, and watched a few movies on demand—*The Black Stallion, National Velvet, The Secret Garden.* I'd seen them all before, but they were like comfort food for my mind. Knowing how they ended made me feel safe and happy. . . .

On the third day of rain I begged Mom to take me to Hillsborough. "There must be a library or a bookstore in town. I don't have anything to read, and Dad's crew is driving me crazy."

"A break's a great idea." Mom pressed Save and shut down her laptop. "The noise is giving me a headache."

She picked up her purse, grabbed her rain jacket, and tossed mine to me. She found the truck keys and headed for the door to tell Dad where we were going.

Reluctantly, I followed her into the house. Now that the plywood was off the windows, a gray, rainy light spilled into the rooms. The crew had pulled up the rotten flooring and put down a solid subfloor. They'd gotten rid of the tree limb and replaced the old stairs to the second floor. They'd swept up dead leaves, fallen plaster, and other trash.

The house smelled like new wood and sawdust. No more musty odor, no mold, no dark, scary corners.

I looked up the stairs toward the third floor. Dad's crew hadn't done any work there, and it was still dark, even in daylight. I sensed Lily hiding behind her locked door, waiting for me to climb the steps, unlock the door, and help her escape from whatever held her there.

If only I had someone who believed in Lily, a friend to climb those stairs with me and save a frightened child.

10

The Girl

The girl in the locked room stands at the window. She spends most of her days here now, watching for the dark-haired girl, who hasn't come outside since the rain began. The things that the girl dug up are lying in a hole filled with muddy water. She can make out the head of the bald doll. One of the doll's arms reaches out of the water, as if she were drowning.

Below her window, the dark-haired girl and her mother hurry through the rain to their tin machine. Their outfits are even more peculiar than usual. The dark-haired girl is wearing a coat so yellow it's blinding. It reminds her of pictures of sea captains steering their boats through stormy weather. She's even wearing the right sort of hat. Oilskins, that's what they're called.

Where on earth does that girl buy her clothing? Surely not in Browne's Emporium.

The mother is dressed in a shiny black belted coat, which looks less strange, but, like the daughter, she's wearing long blue pants. Why do they both dress like boys?

The mother calls, "Jules, watch out for that puddle. It's really deep."

She watches the dark-haired girl hop nimbly over the puddle. *Jules* — is that her name? It's an odd name for a girl, more like a French name for a boy. The world must have changed a great deal since the girl last saw it. Maybe boys wear skirts and play with dolls now. Maybe children take their grandparents for rides in baby buggies.

How silly. She giggles at the very idea.

Even if she dared to leave the room, where would she go in a world so strange? She understands the way things were, not the way they are now.

Jules and her mother get into the tin machine. The engine makes its usual loud noises before they disappear from sight.

The girl prefers a horse and carriage, but perhaps they are no longer in style.

She wonders where Jules and her mother are going.

Perhaps to town.

Town. The girl frowns. What gave her that idea? Has she been to town herself? Maybe. She pictures a narrow, dusty road, with rows of shops and houses on either side. There's a church with a steeple at the end of the street. Horses pull carts and carriages. Other horses are tied to railings. People are laughing and talking.

She holds a man's hand, but she can't see his face, only his dark jacket and trousers. A woman takes her other hand. Her dress is long, and tiny blue flowers dot the cloth.

She looks down at herself and sees a blue dress. On her feet are high-top shoes with buttons.

The girl clings to the hands holding hers. She feels safe with the man on one side and the woman on the other. She doesn't know who they are, but she'd like to stay with them.

The woman says something to her, but her voice is faint and far away, and the girl can't make out the words. She tries to smile, but her lips won't move.

Suddenly the man and woman vanish, and the girl is once more standing alone at the window. The rain still falls. It drums on the roof and gurgles in the gutters and splashes in the puddles.

She looks down at herself and smooths her white nightgown, but it isn't white anymore—it's yellowed and worn so thin it's beginning to fall apart.

Where did her blue dress go? Where did her shoes go? What happened to the man and woman? Where are they?

She goes to the mirror on the wardrobe door. Once, she talked to her reflection as if it were a dear friend, a kindred soul. But as the years passed, cobwebs draped the mirror. Its surface tarnished. Her image slowly faded. Now she sees nothing but a shadowy shape, too vague for her to be sure it's her reflection.

Perhaps she doesn't need to hide. Perhaps no one can see her.

11

Jules

In less than half an hour we were in Hillsborough. Even in the rain it looked like a nice place to live. Picket fences, flowers in gardens and window boxes, brick sidewalks, well-kept old houses with big yards, tree-lined streets.

We passed restaurants and coffee places, small clothing stores, a toy shop, a bookstore, a post office, a couple of banks, and a library. Just about everything a person could want or need was right here.

Mom parked in the municipal lot near the courthouse, and we walked toward the library. She paused to sniff a dense green hedge. "Boxwood," she said. "One of my absolutely favorite smells."

I sniffed too. The leaves had a sort of woody, old-fashioned fragrance. If we ever had a house of our own, I'd make sure Dad planted boxwood.

"I'd love to live in a town like this," Mom said. "It reminds me of where I grew up."

"Has Dad said any more about staying in one place for a while?"

"I've talked to him, but you know how difficult it is to pin him down. Always moving, always looking for something new."

I sighed. Dad would never agree to stay in Hillsborough. Or anywhere else. In another year or so, this town would be another memory.

Mom squeezed my hand. "Don't give up, Jules. I think he's open to the idea this time. I'll keep trying to persuade him. You try too. Together we'll wear him down."

Although I wasn't as hopeful as Mom, I let myself imagine living in one of the big old houses we'd driven past. I pictured a boxwood hedge, a tree tall enough for a swing, my bedroom with big windows and a view of the mountains in the distance. I'd make friends. I'd go to the same school every year. Maybe I'd have a dog or a cat, maybe both — why not? It was just a daydream, after all.

At the library, Mom headed for the history collection, and I went to the area set aside for teens.

I found the science fiction and fantasy shelves and started searching for a book I hadn't read. A girl about my age joined me. She had short brown curly hair and a friendly face.

Peering at me through eyeglasses with large round lenses, she said, "I haven't seen you before. Are you new here?"

Surprised by her friendliness, I nodded.

"My name's Maisie," she said. "Maisie Sullivan. What's yours?"

"Jules Aldridge." I fingered the paperbacks and struggled to carry on the conversation. "Do you read a lot of fantasy?"

"I *devour* fantasy. My favorite author is Diana Wynne Jones. Have you read the Chronicles of Chrestomanci?"

When I shook my head, she pulled three books off the shelf and thrust them at me. "Read them in order. *Witch Week* is my absolute favorite. You'll love them. I've probably read the whole series at least three times."

I studied the covers. "They look good."

"I guarantee you'll read all of them after you finish the first one. Try *The Magicians of Caprona* when you're done with these three."

"What are they about?"

"Enchanters and magic and alternate worlds."

"Alternate worlds—like space travel? And life on other planets?"

"No. It's more like there are lots of different worlds. The Almost Anywheres, they're called. In each one, something happens that didn't happen in the other worlds."

I had no idea what she was talking about. "Like what?"

"Well, suppose the Confederates won the Civil War. That world would split off from our world, and its history from then on would be different from ours."

"So there could be a world where the British won the Revolutionary War or a world where the Nazis won World War Two or —" I stopped and stared at Maisie. "Wait — how many alternate worlds are there?"

"Too many to count." She laughed. "Maybe there's a world where you didn't come to the library today and you never met me."

I leaned against the bookcase. "Stop. You're making me dizzy."

Maisie's face grew serious. "You know what? According to my dad, lots of people, scientists even, believe there really are alternate worlds."

"So it could be true that different versions of you and me, and everyone else, lead different lives in other worlds that are kind of like this one, only different?"

"Apparently — if you believe the theory."

"Do you?"

"Sort of, yes, pretty much. It's like ghosts and unicorns and magic. You can't prove they exist, but you can't prove they *don't* exist either. So why not believe in the Almost Anywheres? It makes life more interesting, I think."

I hugged the books to my chest and said, "I can't wait to read these."

Maisie grinned. "You sound like someone who loves books as much as I do."

"I get teased all the time about being a bookworm. Do you?"

"Just about every day," Maisie said. "Even my own father tells me, 'Get your nose out of that book and help your mother set the table.'"

"We should start a bookworm club."

"We'll call ourselves Worms R Us!" Maisie slapped her palm against mine, and I dropped my armload of books.

While we gathered them up, I hoped I'd found a friend for as long as I stayed in Virginia—which I hoped would be a long, long time. More likely, of course, it would be a year or two at the most. And then goodbye Maisie, goodbye Hillsborough, hello somewhere new.

Maisie sat down at a table, and I took a seat opposite her. "Do you live here in town?" she asked.

"Just outside," I told her. "My dad's fixing up an old house for a big corporation."

Maisie's eyes widened in interest. "Whoa. Is your dad the guy who's restoring Oak Hill?"

"Yes, that's his job. He —"

Maisie interrupted. "Do you actually live in the house?"

"No. In an addition behind it. My dad and his crew are working on the inside of the house now. It will be a long time before it's fit to live in."

Maisie leaned across the table toward me. "Do you know what happened at Oak Hill?"

I fidgeted with my stack of books. It was obvious Maisie knew something I didn't know, something bad, and I wasn't sure I wanted to hear it. Somehow I knew it would be scary, and Oak Hill was scary enough already.

"It was abandoned a long time ago," I said. "Woods grew up around it, and people forgot it was there. Then Stony-brook discovered it and hired Dad. That's all I know."

"Ha. What does some big company like Stonybrook know? Talk to the people who live here. Nobody ever forgot that Oak Hill was there," Maisie said. "It's been our haunted house story for years. Even in my grandma's day, people were scared to go there."

She pulled a pack of gum out of her pocket and offered me a stick. I took the gum, but all I wanted was to hear what Maisie knew about Oak Hill.

"People say," Maisie went on, "that robbers broke into Oak Hill and murdered the family who lived there. A man, his wife, and his daughter. They say the killers were never caught and the bodies were never found, but the family has haunted the house ever since. Lots of kids have seen their ghosts, my brother included—he says if you go inside the house, you never come out. He's heard stories about a hiker who went in there. All they ever found was his hiking boot. Just one. With *blood* on it. You can hear him screaming sometimes when the wind is right. He also says—"

I grabbed Maisie's arm. "Stop it. Just stop it. I knew something bad happened in that house. From the minute I saw it, I *knew*." I was shivering, and my teeth were chattering, and I thought I might throw up.

"What do you mean?"

"I get these feelings. And I see stuff no one else sees."

Maisie's eyes seemed to widen behind her glasses. "What do you mean? Like ghosts or something?"

I hesitated. What if Maisie didn't believe me? What if she thought I was lying? Maybe she wouldn't be my friend, after all.

She leaned closer. "Did you see a *ghost*, Jules?"

A teenager pushing a library cart stopped next to us to shelve some of the books on his cart. I dropped my voice so low Maisie had to lean farther across the table to hear me. "I saw *Lily*."

"Lily? Who's Lily?"

Maisie spoke so loudly the teenager looked at us. "Stop shouting, Maisie," he said. "You want Miss Hopkins to throw you out again?"

"Get lost, Blake," Maisie said.

"*You* get lost." Blake shoved another book into place and moved on. The sound of the cart's squeaky wheels faded as he disappeared between two rows of tall shelves.

"So who's Lily?" Maisie asked.

"The little girl who haunts Oak Hill."

Maisie stared at me, awestruck. "Where did you see her? Were you scared?"

"Mom and I were in the field behind the house. Mom was asleep, but I was awake. All of a sudden I saw this little girl sitting near me, making a clover chain. I didn't realize she was a ghost at first. She looked like a real girl. There wasn't anything scary about her."

"Did your mother see her?"

"No. She was asleep. When she woke up, she said I

dreamed the whole thing. Maybe I did, I don't know for sure, but—"

Maisie interrupted me. "What do adults know? Lily was *real,* Jules. I feel it in my bones." We were almost nose to nose now. "Have you seen anything else?"

"The first night we were here, I saw the Bennett family in the field behind the house. Nobody believed that either."

"*I* believe you," Maisie said.

Encouraged, I told her about the horses and the midden and the dolls and my feeling that Lily was watching me. "I looked up at a window on the third floor—I think it's her room. I swear I saw her, just a glimpse, but definitely her. Then I looked down. There was a key lying in the grass. I think it opens her door."

With a sigh, Maisie sat back in her chair. "Oh, Jules, I am so jealous. I've always, always, always wanted to see a ghost."

"Come to Oak Hill," I said. "And you just might get your wish."

It was a daring thing to say to someone I'd just met. What if she said no, she had lots of friends and she was busy with them most of the time.

But Maisie looked as if she wanted to hug me. "Oh, Jules, I'd absolutely love to see Oak Hill—and Lily. Just say when, and I'll be there!"

Before we could set a date, Mom appeared. "There you are, Jules."

"This is Maisie," I told her. "We've been talking about books."

Mom smiled. "I'm glad to meet you, Maisie." Glancing at the stack of Chrestomanci books, she said, "Oh, my goodness—Diana Wynne Jones. She was my favorite writer when I was your age. I read every one of her books at least twice."

"Maisie recommended them to me," I told Mom.

"You have great taste, Maisie."

"I've read them over and over again," Maisie said. "I adore them."

Mom smiled at Maisie. "Jules and I are about to have lunch at that little café around the corner. Would you like to join us?"

"Oh, yes, that would be great," Maisie said. "They have the best tuna melts in town."

We grabbed our rain gear, checked out our books, and headed for Mandy's Café and Tea Room. All three of us ordered tuna melts. They were just as delicious as Maisie had said they'd be.

While we ate, Maisie told Mom she'd always wanted to see Oak Hill. "My brother and his friends have been there lots of times, but they never took me. That was before

Stonybrook bought the land and found the house and started fixing it up. I guess it's really changed since Joe explored it."

Mom smiled. "Why don't you come over one day next week? My husband will be happy to take you on a tour, and you and Jules can continue your book discussion."

"Maybe she can stay for dinner and sleep over," I suggested.

Maisie gave me a big grin, and I knew I'd said the right thing. We decided that Tuesday of next week would be a good time for Maisie's visit. "We'll pick you up," Mom said. "The roads are a mess from all this rain. You need four-wheel drive to get through the ruts and puddles at Oak Hill."

We drove Maisie home to a big brick house on Third Street. A tabby cat sat on the porch, and a boy's bike lay on the sidewalk. A swing hung from a big tree in the side yard. The house looked friendly, not fancy, but just right. If Dad bought a house for us in the same neighborhood, Maisie and I could walk to school together.

Maisie thanked Mom for lunch and the ride. To me, she said, "I can't wait to see you next week!"

She waved and ran up the sidewalk, mindless of the rain puddles.

"Well," Mom said, "Maisie is delightful. I'm so glad you two got together."

"Me too." I leaned back against the seat. I had a friend. For once, I'd know someone when I started a new school in the fall. I'd ask Maisie what kind of clothes to wear and how to do my hair. I'd fit in right from the first day.

On the way to Oak Hill, I told Mom what Maisie's brother had said. "I told you something terrible happened in that house," I said. "Do you believe me now?"

Mom glanced at me and shook her head. "That's a good example of an urban legend. Every deserted, spooky old house has a story just like it. It's a cliché, Jules."

"But Mom, I've heard things, seen things—"

Mom frowned. "Oak Hill is simply an old, abandoned house. I admit it's creepy, but nobody was murdered there, nobody is buried there, and the Bennetts are not haunting it."

"You have to believe me! The girl I saw in the field, the one you said was a dream—it was Lily Bennett. She's in the house, she—"

Mom braked and pulled to the side of the road. "Stop it, Jules, right now. That sort of talk is irrational. You're just scaring yourself."

"What do you mean? Do you think I'm crazy?"

"No, of course not. Just calm down, think, use your common sense."

"Fine. Believe what you want to believe." I slumped in my seat and turned my face away.

Mom sat behind the wheel as if she'd forgotten how to drive. At last she sighed and started the car. For the rest of the way, we rode in silence.

12

The Girl

That evening, the girl stands at her window and looks down at Jules's window. The room is empty.

She longs to see Jules. There's a place she needs to go, a safe place where people will love and protect her. She thinks Jules might help her find it.

The moon rises slowly behind the mountains. So many moons, she thinks, so many years. So much waiting.

The sky darkens. Colors fade. Stars pop out, just as they always do, just as they always will.

A light goes on in Jules's room. The girl watches her pass the window and get into bed with a book. The girl thinks that she once had a book. Someone read it to her. The person had a deep voice. She sat on his lap and rested her head on his chest, just under his chin. She was safe then.

"When will you unlock my door?" she whispers to Jules. "When will you free me?"

After Jules turns out her light, the girl curls up in her nest in the wardrobe. She strokes the silken rags. She's so tired, but she cannot sleep. How long will she lie here?

13

Jules

That night, I dreamed of the horses again and woke to hear their hooves pounding the ground. On they came, louder and closer than ever before. The men cursed and pounded on the door of the old house. The woman cried out in fear.

Where was Lily? Where were her parents? Why didn't the hired help come to their aid?

Then, as quickly as the riders arrived, they vanished into the dark. Who were they? Why did they come? What did they want?

✦

In the morning, the sun shone and everything sparkled as if it were brand-new. Water drops shone on spiderwebs and blades of grass. Mud puddles reflected the cloudless sky.

To celebrate Dad's day off, we took a slow drive down the Blue Ridge Parkway to Roanoke and ate lunch at a little restaurant in the old part of town. It was too hot for walking, so Dad suggested going to the Taubman Museum of Art to cool off in air-conditioned comfort.

In the American Art section, all three of us stopped in front of a large oil painting. Even though Oak Hill looked very different now, the painting was definitely Oak Hill as it must have been many years ago.

Dad leaned down to read a small plaque on the wall beside it: HENRY BENNETT. OAK HILL, CIRCA 1883. OIL ON CANVAS.

"Isn't that the artist you found on the census?" I asked. "The man who lived at Oak Hill?"

"That's right, Jules." Dad studied the painting. "He was an amazing artist. So much detail, yet not stiff or overdone. His brushwork is especially nice."

"Oak Hill was beautiful then," Mom said. "The house, the trees, the stone walls . . . And those flower gardens. Take a picture of the painting, Ron. Maybe Stonybrook can hire a landscaper to recreate the grounds as they once were."

While Dad got busy with his camera, I studied the painting. A little girl sat in a swing that hung from a tall oak tree. Her hair was blond and her dress was blue. A woman stood behind her, ready to push the swing.

The little girl was definitely Lily, but the woman was too old to be her mother. Maybe she was her grandmother or her aunt. In the background, a younger woman watered the flower garden. Lily's mother, I guessed. Every detail was so perfect, I felt as though — if I tried hard enough — I could step into the picture and visit Lily's world as it was before the robbers came.

I thought of the Chrestomanci books and the Almost Anywheres. What if alternate worlds really existed? Maisie's father said they might. Suppose there was a world where the robbers don't kill the Bennetts, a world where Lily grows up and lives a happy life. Suppose Maisie and I discovered a way to send Lily to that world?

Mom interrupted my thoughts. "Henry Bennett was so talented. It's a shame he's not better known. I wonder what happened to him, why he stopped painting."

Because he was murdered, I wanted to say, just like I told you yesterday. But you didn't believe me then and you won't believe me now. So what's the use of saying it again?

We walked around the room, looking for more of Henry Bennett's paintings, and found a few small landscapes of the Blue Ridge Mountains. While Dad and Mom admired the detail and brushwork, I discovered a picture of Lily making a clover chain. She sat in the field, her doll beside her, just as I'd seen her on the day Mom insisted I'd been dreaming.

Mom paused beside me to look at the painting. She glanced at me, and I hoped she'd say, *Oh, Jules, you really did see Lily.* But no. She frowned and turned her attention to a watercolor of an old barn.

I was disappointed, but I didn't say a word. If the painting didn't convince Mom, she'd never believe I'd actually seen Lily.

✦

On Sunday afternoon, Mom suggested that we have a picnic dinner by the stream. She put me in charge of carrying a chocolate cake she'd gotten from the bakery. Dad was responsible for a heavy picnic basket filled with food and drinks, and Mom carried an old quilt and a bowl of potato salad.

Dad gazed across fields of tall grass and wildflowers rolling off toward the mountains. Here and there, old stone walls and hedges divided the land. "Just look at that view," he said. "I haven't seen anything except that house since we arrived. We should do this every Sunday."

Mom took a deep breath. "The air's so fresh. All I smell is grass and honeysuckle."

Dad grinned. "I could live in a place like this."

I almost dropped the cake. "Dad, do you mean that? We'd stay here and not move anymore? Live like normal people? No more new schools?" In my excitement, my words tumbled over each other.

Dad looked at me. "Well, no, not now, Jules. I was thinking ahead to when I retire."

"Oh." I actually felt my heart drop like a stone.

I looked away, and Mom realized I was upset. Putting an arm around my shoulders, she said, "It would mean so much to Jules, Ron. This area is full of old houses in need of work. Surely you could find enough projects to keep you busy."

Dad turned from the view to look at me. "I'm not promising anything, but I'll take some time to drive around and see what's what." He shrugged. "Maybe it's time to settle down."

I put the cake down and hugged him. "Please, Dad, please."

"Okay, okay, Jules. Like I said, I'll do some reconnaissance."

"Let's not forget what we came here for," Mom said. "We have some serious eating to do."

From the look she gave Dad, I guessed they also had some serious talking to do.

"Please, please, please," I chanted to myself. "Settle down, buy a house, plant boxwood."

We spread the quilt in the willow's shade, and Mom opened the picnic basket. After we'd eaten all we could— which was just about everything—Dad wandered off with his camera, and Mom and I lounged on the quilt, too full to wade in the stream or do anything but lie still and listen to our insides rumble.

I'd brought *The Lives of Christopher Chant* with me, and Mom insisted on reading aloud from it. In the scene she chose, Christopher was in another world, one of many Almost Anywheres. I closed my eyes and surrendered to the magic of the second Chrestomanci book. No matter how old I was, I still loved to listen to Mom read out loud. It freed my mind somehow.

Gradually I realized that Mom's voice had been replaced by a voice softened with a southern accent. The book she read aloud had changed to *Little Women*.

In my drowsy state, the change didn't bother me. I

relaxed and let myself sink into the grass, into the story, into the warmth of the summer day.

A fly buzzed around my face, and I opened my eyes to swat it. A few feet away, a woman sat on a quilt, reading aloud from *Little Women*. Lily lay beside her, the doll nearby. Not far from them, a man stood behind an easel, painting the scene.

Doing my best to ignore the fly, I lay still and listened to Mrs. Bennett read about Beth's death. Mesmerized, I hung on every word of the story, as if I'd never read it.

Lily sat up. Tears ran down her face. "Mama, please stop reading. I don't want Beth to die. It frightens me to think about it." As her mother turned to lay the book aside, Lily looked at me. She saw me just as clearly as I saw her. "Lily," I whispered. "Lily."

She said something that sounded like *Help,* but her voice was low and indistinct, a whisper in a keyhole, a sigh under a closed door, a rustle in the leaves.

I leaned closer to hear better, but the moment I moved, Lily and her mother and father wavered like a reflection in a pond and vanished.

I looked at Mom, hoping she'd seen Lily at last, but she lay on the quilt, sound asleep, the Chrestomanci book facedown on her stomach. Dad slept nearby, snoring softly, a smear of chocolate icing on his upper lip.

The place where I'd seen the Bennetts was empty, the grass undisturbed. But Lily was still here, trapped in the house, waiting for me.

I walked to the stream and sat on the bank. Below my feet, the Gerridae skated in circles, and the minnows flashed beneath them, just as they had when Lily was alive. When Maisie came, we'd find a way to rescue her.

14

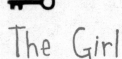

The Girl

The girl sits on the floor watching a bird fly around her room. Birds have come in before. Usually they flap about frantically, seeking a way out.

This bird is different. Instead of being in a hurry to leave, it hops around, investigating things. Perhaps it hopes to find a juicy bug to eat. She would like to help him, but even if there were a bug in her room, lately she's been having trouble picking things up. She's not very strong, perhaps because she hasn't been outside in the fresh air for a very long time. She can't remember when she last ate. She's never hungry, but maybe not eating has weakened her.

She stretches out her arms and looks at them. How thin she's become. Why, she can scarcely see her arms. The sun seems to shine through them, and they cast no shadow.

The girl contemplates the bird. "I wish you'd stay with

me and be my pet," she says. Her voice is low and raspy. Maybe she should talk more. But what's the point of that? She has no one to talk to.

Suddenly the bird spreads its wings and flies out the window. The girl watches it dip and soar, dip and soar, and finally disappear into the woods. If only she could spread her arms and fly after him.

After the bird leaves, she's lonelier than ever. The day before, Jules and her father and mother had gotten into their ugly tin thing and driven away. They were gone all day. She was afraid they might be gone forever, but late at night, she saw the lights of their tin thing. She was glad they'd returned.

Today the three of them left the house again, on foot this time. Jules carried a cake. Cake—she remembers cake. It's soft and sweet; it melts in your mouth. Once, in some other time, she ate cake. Chocolate cake. Outside in a field —a picnic, that's what it's called. There was a stream, a tree, wildflowers, butterflies. She ate until she thought her stomach would burst. Eating like that now might put some flesh on her bones.

Maybe Jules and her parents are having a picnic by that stream with the tree and the wildflowers and the butterflies. She hopes so. It's a happy place. She wishes she could go there herself.

The girl drifts into a dream. She's outside near the stream and the tree, lying on a quilt in soft grass. Someone is reading to her. It's a voice the girl knows and loves. She lies still and listens to a story about four sisters. She's heard it before, but she can't remember what happens to the sisters. She thinks one dies. She remembers crying. She's not sad now. She can't remember what dying is.

In her dream, she senses someone watching her. She turns her head. Jules is there, close enough to touch. She calls her Lily. The girl doesn't know who Lily is. Once, she knew, but it was so long ago, so long ago.

"Help me," the girl hears herself say. "Help me."

Jules doesn't understand her. When Jules moves, she vanishes, the way a reflection vanishes when you toss a pebble into water.

The girl comes to herself by the window. She sees Jules walk out of the woods with her parents. Just there, just below her. She hopes Jules will look up and see her, but she hurries into the house with her mother. She's not thinking about the girl.

The girl sighs and backs away into the shadows. Jules can't help her. No one can.

15

JULES

We came home from the picnic after dark. The shadows made me uneasy. Something screamed in the woods, and I grabbed Dad's hand.

"It's an owl hooting," he said. "A barn owl—the one with the pretty, heart-shaped face and the horrible screech."

I clung to his hand. Owl or not, the cry chilled me through and through. I became intensely aware of every sound—the snapping of a twig, a rustle in the bushes, the wind sighing in the branches. Even the man in the moon looked anxious.

"It's lovely to walk in the night with a full moon to light our way home," Mom said. "It makes me think of Byron's poem—'She walks in beauty, like the night . . .' "

The night didn't make me think of anything but galloping horses and angry shouts. What if the men came upon us here? Would I be the only one to see them? Would my parents believe me if I said we were in danger?

I walked faster, tripping over roots and stones. Mom and Dad urged me to slow down and watch my step, but I walked even faster. And so did they.

When we came out of the woods, I was actually glad to see the dark bulk of the house ahead of us.

It was nine thirty by the kitchen clock. I was too tired to keep my eyes open, so I went to bed. Instead of falling asleep, I lay there thinking of Lily. When I'd called her name, she'd looked right at me. Had she really asked me to help her?

✦

The next morning, after Dad left, I asked Mom if he'd said any more about finding permanent work in Hillsborough.

"We talked last night after you went to bed, but he's still unsure."

"Please make Dad understand how much I want to stay here."

"Your father seems stubborn to you, maybe even insensitive, but I'm sure I can convince him that it's in your best interest."

"Thanks, Mom." I gave her a hug. "I love you so much."

"I love you, too, sweetie." She raised her coffee cup in a salute. "Here's to our permanent home in Hillsborough!"

I clinked my juice glass against it. "To Hillsborough!"

Mom opened her laptop. "I promise I won't give up until your father says yes."

While Mom worked on her novel, I washed the breakfast dishes. The sink was under a window that had a view of the field behind the addition. With my hands in warm soapy water, I watched a doe and a pair of speckled fawns move leisurely through the weeds and vanish into the woods. A pheasant flew up from the underbrush, and three or four vultures circled above the treetops.

Vultures. High in the sky, soaring in circles, they were beautiful. But on the ground, up close, they were downright ugly. Scrawny red necks, black feathers, long, wicked beaks, they hunched by roadsides and gathered around dead animals, ripping them to pieces.

Dad said vultures keep the world clean, but most people saw them as I did—bad omens.

Just as I set the last plate in the dish drainer, a group of men appeared at the edge of the woods. Their clothing was old-fashioned—dark pants, white shirts, black suspenders. They wore wide-brimmed hats. They seemed to be looking for something. The vultures hovered over their heads and watched.

A man shouted to the others. "Oh, Lord, come quickly. I've found them."

"Are they all right?" one called.

"Dead," he cried. "Murdered."

The others rushed to his side and took off their hats. They looked down silently. One of the men groaned. "It's Henry and Laura."

Another said, "But where's their daughter? Where's Lily?"

No one answered. As the vultures circled above them, the men stood silently with their heads bowed.

A second later they were gone. Men and vultures both. I stared at the dark shadows between the trees and twisted a dishcloth in my hands. My legs trembled, and I leaned against the sink to steady myself. What was wrong with me? Was I hallucinating—or was I seeing ghosts from the past?

I backed away from the sink and bumped into a chair. Mom looked up from her laptop. "What's wrong, Jules?"

"Nothing. I just tripped over the chair." To hide my shaking hands, I crammed them into my pockets.

"But you look so pale." She got to her feet and peered at me. "Are you sure you're not coming down with something?"

"I'm fine. Really."

"I was about to fix coffee. Shall I make a cup of tea for you? It'll only take a moment."

"That would be nice." I sat at the table. My legs were still shaking, and my heart was beating too fast. I was surrounded by the ghosts of Oak Hill, and I wanted to know why.

A few minutes later Mom set a teacup in front of me. "I put honey in it."

"Thank you." I picked up the cup and smelled bergamot. Earl Grey, my favorite.

Mom sat beside me. Her laptop was closed. "Something's bothering you, Jules. It's more than the old house, isn't it?"

I stared into my cup. The tea was so clear I saw the flowers on the cup's bottom. "I'm fine, Mom, really."

Mom turned her cup as if it had to be in a certain spot, its handle facing just the right way. Touching it lightly with her fingertips, she said, "Are you still worrying about the Bennett family?"

"Don't you want to know what happened to them?"

Mom sipped her coffee and then set her cup down carefully. "Not really. Some things are best left unknown."

"But what if you could change the past, so what happened in this world didn't happen in another world?"

"Like the Chrestomanci books?"

"Well, yes. What if it's true? What if——"

"Oh, Jules, I love those books as much as you do, but the Almost Anywheres don't exist."

"Maisie's father told her that some people believe in alternate universes. They think——"

"And some people believe the earth is flat." Mom opened her laptop. "Now, I really need to hit the keys. I promised my agent I'd have the manuscript ready last week, and it's still far from finished."

I lingered at the table, wishing Mom had more time to talk, but she was already engrossed in her novel. She wouldn't have believed me anyway.

I walked outside and sat on the deck. Inside, Mom typed away on her laptop. In the old house, Dad and his crew hammered and sawed.

A wind came up. The trees swayed and the sky darkened with heavy clouds. It looked as if it might rain again.

I thought of Lily in her room on the third floor. Was she at her window watching the same stormy sky?

I walked around the house and looked up at her window. Hoping Lily was there, I waved. I glimpsed movement behind the glass. It might have been a response. It might have been a reflection. I waited for a while, but when I saw nothing else, I went back inside and wrote an e-mail to Maisie.

"So much has happened," I told her. "I saw paintings of the Bennetts in a Roanoke museum, then we had a picnic by the stream, and I saw the Bennetts again, all three of them this time. They were having a picnic too, and Lily looked at me and she saw me and said something, but I couldn't understand what — maybe *help*. And then there were these men on the edge of the woods behind the house and they were looking for the Bennetts and they found their bodies, but Lily wasn't with them. Why do I keep seeing these things from the past? I wish you'd been there, Maisie."

16

The Girl

The girl sees Jules wave. In a reckless moment, she waves back. Frightened by what she's done, she ducks away into the shadows. She still isn't sure she wants Jules to see her.

After a while, she crosses the room and looks at the paintings. She's been avoiding them. They make her both sad and angry, a strange mix, she thinks.

Slowly, she turns the ones facing the wall around so she can see the man and the woman. She stares into their painted eyes. They want to speak to her. They have something to tell her. Something important.

She waits patiently for them to open their mouths. She's used to waiting, she's used to being patient. But they remain silent.

She touches their faces. "I'm sorry I don't remember who you are."

They do not answer.

Next she notices a portrait of a yellow-haired girl wearing a pale blue dress. She's sitting in the shade of a tree that has long, drooping branches. Her bare feet dangle over a stream. She holds a doll in her lap. She knows that she has been in that exact place, but she can't remember when.

She stares into the yellow-haired girl's painted eyes. That girl also has something to tell her, but like the man and the woman, she doesn't speak.

"I knew you once," she tells the painted girl, "a long time ago, before . . ." She hesitates. Before what?

She continues to walk around the room, looking at the paintings. Many show the same three people. Some are portraits, and others show the woman and the girl with yellow hair going about their daily life.

She finds several pictures of a house. It might be the one in which she's trapped. Summer, fall, winter, and spring, flowers and gardens and a swing in a tree, snow and bare trees, trees with leaves of gold and red. The artist must have lived in this house once. Why else had he painted it so often?

The girl studies the landscapes. She counts the cows

and the sheep in the pictures. Dim memories stir — the smell of hay in the barn, the large brown eyes of the cows, milk spurting into a pail. The scenes comfort her.

Last of all, she turns to the drawings scribbled on the wall. They're poorly done, childish and clumsy. They tell a story she knew once but doesn't want to know now. They do not comfort her.

She turns away. Her mind is a jumble of half-formed images and memories. Fear hides in the shadows. She wishes she could escape into dreamless slumber.

17

Jules

At last it was Tuesday. I got into the truck with Mom, and we drove to Maisie's house. Mrs. Sullivan met us at the door and welcomed us inside. She was tall and plump, and her hair had turned gray already. It was wild and bushy, untamed. I liked her right away.

"I'm so glad to meet you, Jules." Maisie's mother gave me a hug. "Maisie tells me you love to read. I hope you enjoy those Chrestomanci books as much as she does. Otherwise you'll be sick to death of them long before you've read them all."

"I love them," I assured her. "After I read the last one, I plan to read them all over again."

At that moment Maisie came clattering downstairs, followed by a little girl—her sister, I guessed, because she looked just like Maisie. Maisie was carrying a suitcase and a pillow.

With a huff and a puff she dropped them on the floor. "Hey, Jules, I'm so glad you're here!"

"Are you planning to move in with the Aldridges?" her mother asked.

"Why?"

Mrs. Sullivan laughed. "You've packed so much. That suitcase holds two weeks' worth of stuff."

Maisie looked embarrassed. "Well, a person has to be prepared," she said.

By now the little sister was walking around me, studying me in great detail. "What's your name?" I asked.

"Ellie." She smiled, revealing a big gap where her front teeth used to be. "They both came out at once," she told me. "I tripped over our stupid cat and landed on my face and swallowed them. Not the cat—I didn't swallow her, just my teeth. But the tooth fairy came anyway, which was pretty nice of her, don't you think?"

"Now, Ellie," Mrs. Sullivan said, "don't talk Jules's ear off."

"Could that really happen? Could I talk someone's ear off? Wow. That would be amazing."

Maisie gave her sister a not-too-gentle push. "Get lost, Ellie. We're leaving now."

Ellie laughed. "Don't let the ghosts get you!"

"We'll send them to get *you*," Maisie said.

"I'm not scared of ghosts. If I see one, I'll hit him on the nose and tell him to scram!"

After a round of hugs and a flurry of goodbyes, we got into the truck and left for Oak Hill.

As soon as Mom parked outside the addition, Maisie jumped out and looked at the old house. She must have taken in every detail — the scaffolding the workmen had erected, the sagging roof, the shutterless windows, the weeds growing wild.

Turning to me, she said, "This is so cool. It's like something from a horror movie. I love it."

We followed Mom into the addition, and I led Maisie to my room. She plopped her pillow down on one twin bed and dropped her suitcase on the floor. "Which window is Lily's?"

I pointed. "The little one on the top floor."

Maisie stared so hard I expected the glass to break. "Can you see her? Is she there?"

I joined her at the window. We pressed our faces against

the glass and willed Lily to appear. We even tried chanting her name softly.

Maisie sighed. "I've heard that ghosts only appear to people who don't want to see them."

"That could be true. When we first moved here, I was terrified of ghosts. And then Lily came."

"And you didn't even know she was a ghost at first."

"And when I figured it out, I wasn't scared of her."

Maisie smiled. "Just think, we'll see her together tonight."

We high-fived each other just as Mom called us for lunch, saying, "Dad's made his special grilled cheese sandwiches in Maisie's honor."

After one bite, Maisie told him they were just as good as the tuna melts at Mandy's Café. "Maybe even better!"

"That's a huge compliment," Mom told him.

"Well, the next time I'm in town, I'll be sure to try one," Dad said.

After we'd eaten, Dad asked if we were ready for our tour. Maisie jumped up so fast, she knocked over her glass of cola.

Mom told her not to worry. "Go on," she said. "I'll clean up."

Dad unlocked the door and ushered us into the old

house. The crew was sitting on the parlor floor, eating lunch. Except for their voices, the building was quiet.

As Dad took us from room to room, Maisie stared at the unfinished walls and the roughed-in stairs. She practically sniffed the air for traces of ghosts. The only things I smelled were sawdust and fresh-cut wood.

Dad stopped at the bottom of the stairs. "We have more work to do on the second story, but come on up and take a look. The holes in the floor have been patched, so there's no danger of falling through."

Upstairs, I walked carefully around several stepladders, but Maisie walked under them, as if daring bad luck to find her. We both took care not to trip over tools scattered on the floor and tangles of extension cords snaking everywhere. In the corners, piles of trash waited to be swept up. The crew had left water bottles and soda cans all over the place.

Dad took us through six large bedrooms. Each one had its own fireplace and several big windows, with views of fields and mountains. Even with the walls stripped of plaster, it was easy to imagine how nice the rooms would be when Dad's work was done.

Maisie pointed at a dimly lit, narrow stairway. "What's up there?" she asked.

The hall at the top was dark. I pictured Lily hiding somewhere, her ear pressed to a door, listening to us. Was she afraid of us? Or eager to see us?

Dad shrugged. "Nothing that I know of. We've been hard at work on the first and second floors. A few of the workmen have gone up to take a look. They didn't find anything interesting—just more dirt and rotten floors and spiderwebs."

"Can we see it?" Maisie's foot was already on the first step.

Dad shook his head. "It's not safe, girls. We haven't stabilized the stairs, and the floor's weak."

Maisie and I looked at each other. Tonight we'd see the third floor for ourselves.

Once we were back in my room, I showed Maisie the key I'd found in the midden. She examined it with attention to every detail.

"It's magic," she whispered. "I can feel it. Like something from a fairy tale."

"Not 'Bluebeard,' I hope."

Maisie shuddered, and so did I. Neither of us wanted to find a room full of Bluebeard's dead wives.

"Tonight we'll see if it fits Lily's door," I said.

Maisie looked around my room. "Where are those little dolls you told me about? I'd love to see them."

"I left them in the midden," I confessed. "They scared me."

"How can dolls be scary?"

I put the key back in my box. "Wait till you see the bald one," I said.

18

The Girl

The girl hears Jules's voice. She goes to her window and sees her walking on the grass below. Another girl is with her. Or at least she thinks it's a girl. Her hair is cut shorter than a boy's. Like Jules, she wears boys' short pants and a baggy shirt. A pair of spectacles bigger than Grandfather's perches on her freckled nose.

They stop at the midden. Once more, the girl wonders why Jules is so interested in trash and broken things.

Jules's friend picks up a stick and pokes at the ground. The first thing she finds is the ugly bald doll. "Look at this."

Jules makes a face. "Put her down, Maisie," she says. "That doll scares me."

So the friend is named Maisie. That means she's a girl. Unless boys have girls' names and girls have boys' names. Jules, for instance.

"Not me." Maisie examines the doll. "She must have come from the house. We should keep her."

"You keep her," Jules says. "I don't want her."

The girl watches Maisie lay the doll gently down in the weeds. Why does she want it? It's ugly and ruined. Its eyes are gone, its hair is gone, its body is stained, and its legs and arms are falling off. Jules is right. The doll is scary.

The girl can't bear to look at it. She is sure she doesn't want that doll. It's dead.

Jules sits in the weeds and watches Maisie dig in the dirt. She doesn't help her.

"Oh, look." Maisie scoops up the little china dolls.

The girl's fingers itch to hold them. She has an idea that they're all named Charlotte, but she doesn't know why they share the same name. Such odd notions she has.

She considers making the dolls talk again, but she doesn't want to scare Jules, so she keeps quiet and watches Jules and Maisie divide the little figures between them. The girl wishes they'd share them with her. One for her, that's all. Just one.

Maisie says, "It's hot. Did you say there's a creek where we can cool off?"

The girl watches them disappear into the woods. If only she could go with them. There's something at the end of that path she longs to see. The trouble is, she cannot leave the locked room. She promised not to.

Who made her promise? And why can't she remember?

She looks at the little dolls on the grass, their faces turned up to the sky, their bodies stiff and hard. The bald doll sprawls beside them. A few tufts of hair still cling to her head, and her empty eye sockets are dark holes in her cracked face.

The girl turns away from the window. If she could, she'd run outside and gather all the little dolls and bring them back to her room. She'd play with them. She'd make them talk.

The dead doll can stay where it is. If the girl had a shovel, she'd bury it so deep, no one would ever dig it up again.

19

Jules

Sometime around midnight, when I was sure Mom and Dad were asleep, I led Maisie to the door that opened into the old house. We paused on the threshold and switched on our flashlights. For a moment we stood still and listened.

The house was dark and silent. Nothing moved. Dim light fell through the windows in the parlor.

Maisie took my hand, and we stepped into the shadows. In the darkness, the past reclaimed the house. No matter what Mom believed, I knew people had been murdered in these rooms. Blood had stained its floor. Silent screams hung in its air.

Staying close to Maisie, I forced myself to take one small step and then another. Each step led me farther from the addition and deeper into the old house. No matter how light we were on our feet, the floor creaked under us.

"Are you scared?" Maisie asked.

I shook my head. Actually, I wasn't as scared as I thought I'd be. Maisie made me braver — she wasn't afraid, so I wouldn't be afraid either.

Maisie swept the darkness with her flashlight. Its beam of light made the shadows jump and move. Drafts of night air crept across the floor and chilled my ankles. A shadowy shape scurried across the floor and disappeared into a hole. A mouse? A rat?

I shivered and edged closer to Maisie. Upstairs, Lily was waiting. Perhaps she heard us tiptoeing through the house and knew we were coming to rescue her. For good luck, I touched the key in my pocket.

We climbed the stairs to the second floor, stopping every time a step creaked under our feet. No one heard us, no one called out from the shadows. I tried to breathe slowly and evenly, but I couldn't control the loud thumping of my heart. I'm not afraid, I told myself. I'm brave like Maisie. Lily is waiting. She needs us.

At the bottom of the stairs to the third floor, Maisie touched my arm. Her fingers were so cold I jumped.

"Your hand's like ice," I said.

"It's freezing in here." She put her foot on the first step.

The stairs tilted to one side and the hand railing was loose, so we climbed even more slowly than before. The steps groaned and wobbled, but we kept going.

At the top, I leaned against a wall to catch my breath. Beside me, Maisie breathed hard. "I don't like this place," she whispered.

"I don't either." I looked behind me into the darkness below. Cold sweat ran down my spine. My legs felt so weak I was afraid I'd lose my balance and fall down the stairs.

Maisie turned as if to go back down. "This was a bad idea."

I grabbed her arm to stop her. "We can't leave now. Lily needs us."

Maisie pulled away from me. "You can stay if you like, but I'm getting out of here."

I stared at her in disbelief.

"Come on, Jules, let's go!"

"This was your idea, Maisie. You said nothing scared you."

"Well, I was wrong." Maisie looked as if she were about to cry. "I'm sorry, Jules, but I can't do this."

Just as I was about to follow her back to the addition, the sound I'd been dreading stopped me. "It's the horses," I whispered. "I hear them. They're coming."

"What should we do?" Maisie grabbed my hand and held it tightly.

"If we lock ourselves in Lily's room, the men can't get us."

"Are you sure?"

"It's always the same. The men go into the house, they come back out, and then they ride away. If they could get into her room, they'd take Lily and they wouldn't come back."

Somewhere in the night, very close by, a horse whinnied and a man yelled.

"There's not much time, Maisie, come on!"

We ran to the closed door at the end of the hall. My fingers shook so badly, I dropped the key. Maisie picked it up and handed it to me. She aimed the flashlight at the door while I poked the key at the keyhole. No matter which way I turned it, I couldn't fit it into the lock. My heart banged like a demented thing and my breath came in gulps. It didn't help that Maisie's hands shook so hard she couldn't hold the flashlight steady.

"Hurry up," Maisie begged. "They're coming—give me the key. Get out of the way, let me try."

As Maisie tried to push me aside, the key turned with a loud, grating sound. I grabbed the knob, but my hands were so sweaty and shaky I couldn't get a good grip on it.

"Hurry up, open the door!" Maisie cried. "They're in the yard!"

"Help me. It's stuck."

Together we pushed against the door. It opened so quickly we tumbled into the room and sprawled on the floor.

As soon as I'd locked the door behind us, the men came running up the stairs. "Let us in!" they shouted. "We know you're in there!"

Shaking with fear, Maisie and I cowered together, our arms around each other. The men had scared me when they were outside and I was safe in my bed, but to be this close to them reduced me to absolute terror. The wood groaned under their blows. The door shook in its frame. They'd break it down at any moment and find us.

From outside, a woman cried, "Leave the girl be, come away, come away. You've got what you came for."

The men kicked the door, they cursed and swore, but the woman called again and again.

"Fool of a woman," one muttered. "Just wait till I get my hands on her. She'll shut her mouth or I'll shut it for her."

"We'll be back," the other yelled at the door. "You ain't seen the last of us."

With that, they ran downstairs and out the back door. A few moments later they mounted their horses and rode away. Gradually their shouts faded into the dark, and the night was silent.

Maisie and I huddled together and gasped for breath. We were both crying.

Maisie clutched at me with shaking hands. "Are they gone?"

"Yes."

"Are you sure?"

"I told you, Maisie, they won't come back until tomorrow night."

Maisie wiped her nose with the back of her hand. "I'm scared to stay here. Let's go back to your room."

"We don't need to be scared now. Nothing's here but Lily, just Lily."

Maisie took several deep breaths and peered into the darkness. The only light came from the moon. The rest of the room was hidden in shadows. She didn't say anything, but at least she'd stayed with me.

I groped in the dark and found the flashlight she'd dropped. Its beam lit an easel in the center of the room. Beside the easel was a table covered with art supplies — a palette encrusted with dried paint, jars of brushes and pencils, bottles of turpentine, varnish, and ink, tubes of oil paint, sticks of charcoal, and stacks of drawing paper.

If it hadn't been for the thick gray fur of dust coating everything, I would have expected Mr. Bennett to return at any moment and finish the painting on the easel.

"Jules!" Maisie gasped and grabbed my arm. "There's someone over there, looking right at us."

I swung the flashlight and saw a man's face peering at us from the shadows. I staggered back in fright and bumped into something that fell over with a clatter. A lot of other things followed it, hitting the floor like a row of dominoes.

"It's a painting," Maisie cried in relief. "They're all paintings."

Laughing like loud, silly kids, we saw dozens of paintings leaning against the walls. Several more lay on the floor where they'd fallen after I'd knocked over the first one.

It was like being in an art gallery. Landscapes, animals, portraits. Dad was going to be so excited to know they were here, hidden in this house for over a hundred years, but still as beautiful as the day Henry Bennett painted them.

"My mother does watercolors of flowers," Maisie said, "but this is real art."

We stopped in front of a large painting of a girl sitting

on a tree limb, her bare feet dangling over a stream. The sun backlit her hair and illuminated each strand so it haloed her face. Her father had caught the life in her eyes and dotted her nose with freckles. She was so alive, I almost expected her to speak to us.

"This must be Lily," Maisie whispered.

"Yes," I said, and I leaned closer. "Lily Bennett is sitting exactly where I've sat. Isn't that amazing?"

"Look at the doll she's holding, Jules. It must be the one we found in the midden. I told you it belonged to Lily."

"It looked a lot better when it was new," I said.

"Are these her parents?" Maisie pointed at the portraits on either side of Lily. On the right was a woman, her face slightly turned toward a window. She wore a long lavender dress, and her dark hair was swept back into a loose twist.

On the left was a man sitting behind an easel, peering around the back of a canvas, as if he were looking into a mirror and painting his reflection. He held a brush in one hand. His palette lay on the table beside him.

"It's Henry and Laura Bennett," I said. "Without a doubt."

Behind us, I heard a faint rustling, as if we'd frightened a mouse. I looked at the wardrobe in the corner. The sound had come from there, I was sure of it.

I glanced at Maisie to see if she'd heard anything, but she was still looking at the painting of Lily sitting on the tree limb.

"Oh, Lily," she whispered, "please don't hide. Come out and talk to us."

20

Lily

The men are gone, but Jules and Maisie are in the studio. The girl wanted them to come, and here they are, but she's afraid to let them see her. Her nightgown is tattered and yellow with age. Her hair is long and tangled. She has no shoes.

The girl peeks through a crack in the wardrobe's door. Jules and Maisie have stopped in front of a picture of the yellow-haired girl, the very picture she herself looked at just the other day. If only she knew who that yellow-haired girl is. Her name is on the tip of the girl's tongue. That's something people say when they forget things. She remembers an old woman saying, "Oh it's on the tip of my tongue. Drat. Why am I so forgetful?"

Who was that old woman?

The girl returns her attention to the two friends. Maisie says something to Jules in a low voice.

In a louder voice, Jules says, "Yes." She leans closer to the painting. "Lily is sitting exactly where I've sat. Isn't that amazing?"

The girl trembles when she hears Jules say *Lily*. The name lingers in the air, it echoes in the girl's head, sparks fly up—*Lily, Lily, Lily*. Could it be *her* name? Could she be Lily?

"Yes," she whispers, "yes." Jules has given her something she lost a long time ago. Her name. Lily.

She hugs her name close to her heart and says it over and over. She mustn't forget it again. A dam has broken, and her memories are pouring over it, filling her head with so many forgotten things. She is Lily. She's six years old. She lives in Oak Hill. The doll in the painting is the one Jules dug up in the midden. The doll was new then, a birthday present from Grandmother Pettifer, the old lady who forgot things.

How did her favorite doll end up in the midden? Who threw it there? Surely not Lily herself.

And what happened to the doll to make her so ugly, so dead?

Lily shivers. There's something she knows but doesn't want to know. It hides in the shadows with her, dark and dangerous. She keeps her back to it. She will not face it. But it reaches for her, it whispers. She plugs her ears with her fingers and keeps her mind focused on the girls. She will not listen to the story the darkness whispers.

Jules tells her friend that the man and woman in the other paintings are Lily's parents, Laura and Henry Bennett.

More memories flood back. Mama's and Papa's faces float before her in the darkness, and Papa looks out from the portrait he painted of himself.

At the sight of them, Lily feels a fierce stab of pain. She retreats to the back of the wardrobe and burrows into the rags of her mother's dresses. She's a mouse, tiny and helpless and all alone. She's been abandoned. Left behind. Unloved. Forgotten.

Why is she not with Mama and Papa?

The voice in the dark speaks into her ear. She cannot block it out. She presses her fist to her mouth and sobs quietly. It's not just sorrow she feels, it's also rage. They locked her in this room and never came back. Her own mama and papa. She loves them so much, it hurts to remember them.

Jules's and Maisie's voices interrupt her thoughts. They've found the drawings on the wall.

"They tell a story," Jules says.

Yes, they tell a story. Oh, yes, they do. Like everything else Lily's forgotten, the story comes back to her.

21

Lily

The story those pictures tell begins on a sunny morning with the promise of a picnic. Usually Aunt Nellie prepares the food, but when Lily comes downstairs, Aunt Nellie isn't in the kitchen. She hasn't set the table for breakfast. Lily doesn't smell bacon or freshly baked bread or coffee.

"Where is Aunt Nellie?" she asks Mama. "Why isn't breakfast ready?"

Papa is standing at the window, his back to her. Mama is beside him. Lily's question startles them. They turn and look at her, as if they're surprised to see her.

"It's Nellie's day off," Papa says quickly.

"But today is Saturday," Lily says. "Aunt Nellie's day off is Sunday."

"Aunt Nellie had something important to do," Papa says. "So she asked to have today and tomorrow off."

Mama frowns at Papa, as if she wants to say something, but she reaches for Lily's hand instead. Lily senses something between her parents—a worry they aren't sharing.

"What did Aunt Nellie need to do?" Lily doesn't like not knowing things. Surely if she asks enough questions, Papa will tell her where Aunt Nellie is. He must know. The cook is almost part of the family, not really an aunt, but like an aunt. Papa's secretive air is worrisome.

His face reddens. "For heaven's sake, stop asking so many questions. I don't know why she wanted two days off or what she planned to do. And stop calling her your aunt. She's no relation to you."

Lily draws back, shocked at his tone of voice. Papa is never cross with her. Why must she stop calling Aunt Nellie her aunt? She should be quiet, but she hasn't asked the most important question.

She turns to Mama this time. "How will we have a picnic if Aunt Nellie isn't here to fix the food?"

Mama straightens the ribbon in Lily's long hair. "Don't worry. We don't need Nellie. You and I will roll up our sleeves and put on aprons and do the cooking ourselves. Won't that be fun?"

Lily is puzzled. "Cooking is Aunt Nellie's job. I've never seen you cook anything."

Out of the corner of her eye she sees Papa frown, probably because she forgot and said "Aunt Nellie." Mama touches his sleeve, as if to say *Be quiet, let her call the woman aunt if she wants to.*

Papa shrugs, but he doesn't smile. He turns to look out the window, as if he expects to see someone approaching the house.

Mama ties a huge apron around Lily's waist. Aunt Nellie is a big woman, both taller and heftier than Papa. The apron Mama chooses for herself is also too big.

While she and Mama begin to assemble ingredients, Papa fetches his drawing pad and sketches them at work. Neither Mama nor Lily has had much experience in the kitchen. They spill flour and sugar. A pot of melted chocolate tips over on the table, and Lily scoops it up with a spoon, which she licks clean. Mama drops three eggs. The yolks break and run into the whites.

One of the eggs has blood in it, and Lily turns away. The blood means that the beginning of a baby chick was in that egg.

Papa cleans up the eggs and throws the mess out the back door.

When they've finished the cooking and baking, Mama packs a picnic basket with roast chicken, potato salad, green beans, lemonade, and a big, beautiful lopsided chocolate cake.

Before they leave the house, Papa shows them the sketches he's drawn. "I'm calling these drawings *Amateurs in the Kitchen*," he says.

Mama laughs. "How about *Cook's Day Off*?"

Lily says, "I hope Aunt Nellie comes back soon or we'll starve to death."

She notices Mama and Papa exchange another look that she can't interpret. What do they know and why don't they tell her?

Mama holds out a hand for Lily to take. "Come along."

She clasps Mama's hand and decides to put Aunt Nellie out of her mind. For the moment at least.

They take a path through the woods and across a field to a shady spot by a stream. Mama carries the picnic basket, and Papa carries a patchwork quilt. Lily runs ahead. Grown-ups are so slow. Bees buzz in clover growing tall on the edges of the field. Lily sees a monarch butterfly flying ahead of her, as if it's leading her somewhere.

Under the shade of a willow tree, Mama spreads the quilt on the grass, and Lily helps her unpack the basket. She'd eaten only one of yesterday's biscuits and an apple for breakfast because she's saving her appetite for the picnic, especially the chocolate cake. She smells roasted chicken, and her empty stomach rumbles so loudly that Papa looks around and says, "Is that a bear growling?"

Lily giggles. She eats both chicken wings and a drumstick, a big serving of potato salad, a smaller serving of slightly burned green beans, and an enormous piece of chocolate cake.

Her stomach full to bursting, she lies on her back and peers up at the canopy of leaves shushing and fluttering overhead. It's as if the leaves are sharing secrets with each other. She can't remember a better day than this one.

After a while Mama begins to read aloud from *Little Women*. Lily is drowsy from the food and the summer heat. She begins to fall asleep, but she has the oddest feeling that someone is watching her. She opens her eyes and turns her head to the side.

For a moment she sees a dark-haired girl looking at her. The girl says something Lily cannot understand. Lily tries to speak, but her voice is too small for anyone, even herself, to hear. She blinks, and when she opens her eyes, the girl is gone. Too tired to tell anyone about the girl, Lily closes her eyes. Soon she is fast asleep.

When Lily wakes, Mama allows her to take off her shoes and wade in the stream. She steps into the water and shivers at its icy touch. The sand on the bottom is smooth and feels soft under her feet. She splashes and laughs when she realizes that the skirt of her dress is soaked.

The willow casts its shade on a still part of the stream. Small insects with long, skinny legs walk across the water's surface. They move like skaters, darting quickly from here to there, leaving faint circles behind them.

"Papa," she calls. "What are these odd bugs called?"

He squats down and peers at them. "They're part of the Gerridae family," he tells her, "but most people call them water walkers, water striders, pond skaters, and so on. Fascinating, aren't they?"

Lily trails her hand through the water, taking care not to disturb the gerry bugs. "I wish I could walk across the stream on tiny feet like theirs," she says. "It would be fun, wouldn't it, Papa?"

She watches a bird soar overhead. "Flying would be fun too."

"Oh, Lily." Papa smiles. "Such a fanciful child you are."

Mama joins Papa and looks down at her. "Your toes are turning blue with cold," she says. "You'd better come out and put on your shoes and stockings before you catch a chill."

Lily sits on the grass and spreads her wet skirt around her. It's late in the afternoon, and the sun hovers like a golden ball above the treetops.

The happiness she felt earlier bubbles up inside and she smiles at a rabbit hopping across the field. Papa coughs, and the rabbit freezes, as if he thinks no one will see him if he doesn't move. The sun shines through his ears and dyes them pink. His nose twitches. Papa coughs again, and the rabbit bounds away. A patch of weeds quivers to mark his hiding place, but the rabbit is now truly invisible.

The rabbit is smart. No one will catch him. He knows how to be still and how to hide.

Mama wipes chocolate off Lily's mouth with her handkerchief. "The cake is a sorry mess in comparison with Aunt Nellie's creations," she says.

Papa cuts a big slice for himself and divides what's left between Mama and Lily. "The best cake I ever ate," he tells Mama. "Ten times better than any of Nellie's finest concoctions."

Mama smiles and blushes. "Fibber," she whispers.

Papa gives her a kiss on the cheek. "I'd never lie to you."

"Would you lie to me?" Lily asks.

"Never." Papa stretches and gazes across the fields, which are lush with wheat. Cattle moo. Up on the hillside, sheep answer with bleats. A flock of starlings settles in a tree for the night, disturbing the quiet with their harsh cries.

"Then tell me where Aunt Nellie's gone and when she'll be back." Lily is taking a chance. Papa might not answer. He might be cross. But Lily has to know.

Papa looks at Mama, who says, "You might as well tell her, Henry."

"Lily, you know Mr. Bailey is a hard man to deal with. He doesn't do the work I pay him for. He lies. He mistreats his wife and the animals in his care."

Papa looks into Lily's eyes. She knows he's telling the truth.

"Yesterday I caught him stealing money from the cash box—over five hundred dollars that I forgot to put in the safe."

Papa frowns. "I fired him, and the hired hand quit. This morning I discovered that they stole three of our horses last night and rode off. Nellie went with them." He wipes his sweaty forehead. "I hope we don't see any of them again."

"Aunt Nellie didn't want to go," Lily says. "He made her, I know he did. She's scared of him, Papa. She does what he tells her."

Papa takes her hand in his big hand. His love flows from

his hand to hers and warms her. He looks at Lily, as if she knows something she isn't supposed to know.

"He hits her." Lily says this so quietly Papa doesn't hear. He must have noticed that Aunt Nellie's eye was black last week. The week before that, she had bruises all over her arms. Who would have hit her but Mr. Bailey?

With a sigh, Mama gets to her feet and begins to gather up the picnic things. Papa shakes out the quilt, and Lily helps him fold it. The sun is sinking into a bed of pink and purple clouds, and the evening air is chilly. It's time to leave the stream and the water striders behind.

"We should do this every week," Mama says.

"Yes, yes, let's!" Lily claps her hands and laughs. She's glad to have something else to talk about.

"Why not every *day*?" Papa asks.

"Can we start tomorrow?"

Papa lifts her above his head, and her hair tumbles down over his face.

"Oh, Papa," she says, "I love you so!" Turning to Mama, she adds, "And I love you too, Mama, forever and ever and ever!"

By the time they come in sight of the tall stone house on the hill, it's almost dark. The moon lights their way across the fields and along the path. The evening damp breathes out the scent of grass and wildflowers. In the woods, tree frogs call, and in the distance an owl hoots.

Papa carries Lily upstairs to bed. Mama helps her change into her nightgown. She and Papa kiss her goodnight and tuck her in. Lily wants to hear another chapter of *Little Women*, but she's too tired to keep her eyes open.

22

Lily

B ut that's not the end of the story. It's just the end of the happy part.

The noise of galloping horses wakes her from dreams of picnics and chocolate cake. She opens her eyes and sees Mama standing by the bed, her face barely visible in the dark.

Startled, Lily sits up, wide-awake. She grasps her mother's hand and senses her fear. Why is someone coming to call so late at night? Who is it? What do they want? She's frightened.

Mama pulls Lily out of bed. "Quick," she whispers. "Run upstairs to Papa's studio. Don't make a sound. Lock the door behind you. Hide in the wardrobe, and don't come out until Papa and I come for you."

As Mama speaks, someone pounds on the kitchen

door. A man shouts, "Let us in, Bennett, we've got business to settle."

Papa says something, and Lily hears the door burst open and bang against the wall. A man in heavy boots barges into the house, cursing and yelling. Another follows him.

"Get out of my house, Bailey. You're out of your mind with drink," Papa says. "Go home, sleep it off, or I'll report you to the sheriff."

Lily clings to Mama. "What does Mr. Bailey want?"

"Don't worry. Your papa will take care of it."

"I'm afraid," Lily whispers. "Please let me stay with you."

Mama rushes her toward the stairs to the third floor. "Do as I say, Lily. I'll explain later."

Downstairs, something heavy crashes to the floor. Glass breaks. The noise is terrifying.

Mama shoves Lily toward the stairs. "Go," she whispers. "Go now!"

Mama sounds angry. Whimpering with fear, Lily does as she's told. Her legs are weak. Her bare feet make no noise.

In silent haste she slips into Papa's studio and locks the door behind her. The smell of oil paint and turpentine mixes with the odor of Papa's pipe. The familiar aroma makes it seem as though Papa is in the studio, playing hide-and-seek with her.

Lily obeys Mama and hides in the wardrobe. She ducks under Mama's old dresses and curls up in the back, where the shadows are darkest. No one will find her here. She's a mouse, a rabbit, a tiny creature that knows how to be still.

The noise downstairs grows louder. The men's voices rise. Mama screams and screams again. Lily hears explosions, two, three, maybe more. She recognizes the sound of gunfire. There's more cursing, more thuds and bangs.

She whimpers and burrows deeper into the dresses. The fragrance of Mama's scent lingers in the silk, but Lily doesn't feel safe now. Something is terribly wrong.

From the yard, Aunt Nellie cries, "You drunken fools, what have you done?"

"Where's the girl?" Mr. Bailey shouts. His voice comes from Lily's bedroom on the floor below.

He runs up the stairs. Someone is with him. Not Papa. It must be Ellis Dixon.

They stop at the locked door and struggle to open it. They throw themselves against it.

Where is Papa? Why doesn't he stop them? She wants to call him, but she forces herself to be quiet. One sound, and they'll find her.

"Open the door, Lily," Mr. Bailey shouts. "We won't hurt you."

She hears the anger in his voice. He's lying. If she opens the door, he'll hurt her. He'll beat her with his fists the way he beats Aunt Nellie. Her face will be bruised like Aunt Nellie's, both her eyes will be black, her head will hurt, he might even kill her.

Lily presses her hands over her heart in hope that she can keep the men from hearing it beating so fast and loud. Papa will come soon. He must.

Aunt Nellie shouts again. Her voice shakes with fear. "Please, please. You got what you came for. Forget the child. She's done you no harm. Leave her be!"

Why is Aunt Nellie here? Why doesn't she fetch the sheriff?

Aunt Nellie is afraid of Mr. Bailey. That's why she doesn't get help. No matter how much she loves Lily, she'll do what her husband tells her to do. She always does.

One of the men kicks the studio door so hard, it flies open. They're in the room now. She smells tobacco and whiskey and perspiration. She smells anger and hate, too. In the yard, Aunt Nellie cries, "What are you doing up there?"

"She ain't here, Charlie," Ellis Dixon says. "She's probably hiding in the woods or something. Come on. Let's go while we can. We got the money."

Ellis Dixon runs down the steps, but Mr. Bailey closes the studio door and locks it from the outside. "By the time you get it open," he shouts, "we'll be long gone!"

Downstairs, the men drag things out of the house. Large bundles, maybe. She hears thumps.

"Oh, no, no, no," Aunt Nellie cries. "You promised not to—"

"Shut your mouth!" There's a loud smacking sound, and Aunt Nellie cries out in pain.

"You say one word about what's happened here, and I'll kill you," he yells at Aunt Nellie. "You know I will."

"Charlie!" Ellis Dixon shouts. "Give me a hand. I need some help."

Long after the horses gallop away, Lily stays in the wardrobe and waits.

Where are Mama and Papa? Why don't they come? Perhaps the men tied them up. Surely they'll get loose soon and rescue her.

But the house is quiet. No boards creak. No one climbs the stairs. No one speaks. No one calls her name. It's as if no one is here, no one at all—except Lily.

At last the morning sun slants through the window and pokes fingers of light under the wardrobe door. Lily stays where she is. Her body is stiff and cramped from huddling in the same position for so long, but she obeys Mama and waits.

She's hungry and thirsty. She cries. Have Mama and Papa forgotten her?

They do not come that day. But someone else does. More men tramp through the house. They call her name, but she doesn't recognize their voices. She's afraid they've come to harm her.

She doesn't answer the men, and she doesn't open the door. She promised to wait for Mama and Papa. A promise cannot be broken. No matter what.

After they leave, she selects a stick of Papa's charcoal and begins to draw on the wall. Her hand moves rapidly. She tells the story in pictures. It's not her best drawing, but she's in a hurry. She must not forget what happened.

When she comes to the end of the story, she feels as hollowed out as a dead tree. She's also very tired. So tired. She makes her way to the wardrobe on legs that barely hold her up. She crawls inside and burrows into her mother's dresses. She breathes in her mother's perfume. She falls into a deep sleep.

23

Jules

When we'd looked at the last picture, Maisie turned to me and said, "The drawings tell what happened the night Lily's mother and father were killed."

"If she hadn't hidden in this room, Lily would have been killed too."

I reached for Maisie's hand, and she gripped mine tightly. The shadows darkened and closed in on us. For a moment I felt as if we were trapped just as Lily had been. I shared her fear and loneliness. I understood what it was like to wait for someone who never came, to be locked in a room while outside, the world went on, years passing, season after season coming and going, to hear the horses galloping out of the night, ridden by killers who were searching for you.

Behind us, something creaked, and the spell broke. We turned to look at the wardrobe.

Still holding hands, we crept closer. "Lily—" I called. "Don't be afraid."

No one answered.

"Do you remember the day we saw each other? We were in the field near the stream where the willow tree is. You looked right at me and asked me to help you."

"You *saw* me?"

Maisie and I stared at each other in disbelief. Lily had answered us. She was here in the same room as we were, hidden in the wardrobe, close enough for us to hear her whispery voice.

"What did I look like?" She sounded frightened.

It was an odd question, but I answered as best as I could. "Like the pictures your father painted of you—a pretty little girl with long yellow hair, wearing a blue dress. You were as solid and real as I am."

Lily sighed with what sounded like relief. "I was scared I'd be ugly."

"Ugly? How could you be ugly?"

"Never mind," Lily said. "I saw you too, but I thought I was dreaming."

"You asked me to help you," I said. "Do you remember?"

"It was wrong of me to ask," Lily said. "I have fearful enemies, wicked men—fiends from the devil himself—

in search of me. They'll harm anyone who gets in their way."

"But it's not just those men you need to fear," I told her. "Soon the workmen will start working on the third floor. They'll rip out everything. You won't have a door or a wardrobe to hide in. We have to find another safe place for you."

"You don't understand," Lily said. "I promised Mama I'd stay here until she and Papa came for me. I cannot disobey them."

"Lily, do you know why your mother and father haven't come?" I asked.

Lily was silent for so long I thought she'd never answer, but at last she said, "Yes, I know why. But a promise is a promise, isn't it? It would be wrong to disobey."

"Your parents didn't want you to stay in this room forever, Lily." I laid the key on the floor near the wardrobe. "The door is unlocked. Come with Maisie and me. You can't stay here. We'll find a new hiding place."

"Please don't lock your door, Lily," Maisie begged. "Meet us tomorrow in the field by the willow tree. You know the place."

"We'll keep you safe," I promised.

Lily was quiet again. "It would be nice to sit under the willow again and watch the minnows and the gerry bugs in the stream."

"Then come and meet us, Lily," I said. "We'll find a way to help you."

She paused to think about what we'd told her. At last she said, "I'll meet you tomorrow. I promise." Her voice shook, but she sounded as if she meant it.

We pressed our hands against the wardrobe door and whispered goodbye. "We'll see you tomorrow, Lily. Don't worry, you'll be safe with us."

We ran down the stairs and through the house. In my haste, I tripped over an extension cord and landed on my hands and knees. Maisie helped me to my feet. With a bleeding knee, I hobbled into the addition and the safety of our kitchen.

Once I'd bandaged my cut and we were safe in bed, Maisie asked, "Where are we going to hide Lily?"

I took a deep breath. "I have an idea." I looked at her, worried about her reaction. "If you promise not to laugh, I'll tell you."

Maisie stared at me. "I won't laugh, I promise."

I smoothed the Band-Aid on my knee. "You might think I'm crazy, I don't know, but remember when you told me that some people believe alternate worlds might really exist?"

Maisie frowned. "Yes, but —"

"Well, what if Lily could go to a different world, a world where her parents don't die and neither does she?"

Maisie thought about it. "But the world where she doesn't die," she said slowly, "can't exist until she changes what happened that night."

"Suppose she didn't hide," I said. "Suppose she came downstairs and saved her parents?"

"Like she got a gun and shot Mr. Bailey and Ellis Dixon," Maisie said.

"I can't see Lily doing that."

"How about she spills a big bag of marbles on the floor and the men slip on them and fall and her father gets their guns and calls the police."

"What if Lily doesn't have any marbles?"

Maisie frowned and ran a hand through her hair. "Okay, Jules, what do *you* think she should do?"

"In the picture story, Lily drew a woman outside with the horses. She's the one who cries out on the nights I hear the horsemen. Maybe she'd help Lily. . . ."

"Yes," Maisie said. "Lily can run out of the house and cry for help—"

"And the woman can fetch the sheriff or stop the men or something."

"Do you think it will work?"

"I hope so," I said. "I can't think of anything else. Can you?"

"No," Maisie whispered.

Exhausted, we tried to sleep. Above us, Lily's window was dark, but I sensed her pacing around her room, frightened, confused, worried. She must not know what to do. Stay and obey or leave and disobey. For the first time, I realized what I'd asked Lily to do. She hadn't been out of that room for more than a hundred years. It was all she knew, her safe place. Leaving it must terrify her. No mother, no father to comfort her. No familiar places for her to take shelter from Mr. Bailey and Ellis Dixon.

Maybe it was wrong to ask her to gamble her life on a crazy idea that might not work. But what else was she to do?

In the other bed, Maisie was snoring softly, but I was still awake when the morning light crept in through the skylight and chased the shadows from their corners.

24

Lily

After Jules and Maisie leave, Lily opens the wardrobe door and peers out. Sure enough, the key is on the floor. And the door to her room is open.

With some difficulty, she picks up the key. Her fingers don't work as well as they used to. Indeed, she has become rather clumsy.

She studies the key. As Maisie said, she can lock herself in the room again. Or maybe, if she's brave, if she dares, if she trusts Jules, she can leave.

She tiptoes to the open door. With the key in one hand and her other hand on the doorknob, Lily considers. She's been in this room for a long time, hours and days and weeks, and years—too many to reckon up. She's waited for Mama and Papa. She's done what she was told to do.

She knows why they never came back. They're dead;

they've been dead since the night she locked herself in this room. If she stays here, she'll never see them again.

How does she know this? Because they're dead, and now she knows what that means. And she's still alive. Well, not exactly alive. But not exactly dead either. It's as if she's been forgotten, left behind, with no way to go forward or backward. She's trapped in a world that exists for no one but her and the killers who come for her.

What will happen if she leaves the room? She takes a step over the threshold and then takes a step backwards into the room. She wishes she knew what Papa and Mama want her to do, but they've been gone too long for her to ask. They have no more substance than a shaft of sunlight.

Lily looks out the door again. The hall is empty. It leads to the steps. What will she see if she goes downstairs? Her legs tremble, and she holds fast to the doorframe to keep from falling. She's afraid of what she'll find in the house.

While she hesitates, the sun comes up and paints in the colors that night took away. The workmen arrive. Their laughter booms in the empty rooms, their voices bounce from wall to wall, their heavy boots tramp back and forth on the floor beneath her. Doors open and slam shut.

She creeps to the top of the stairs and pauses there. She

holds her breath. Her toes grip the edge of the first step. She's poised like a diver ready to plunge into deep water.

She lowers one foot, then the other, slow baby steps. She's afraid the stairs will creak, but the wood is silent under her bare feet.

On the second floor, she stops and stares about in bewilderment. The furniture is gone. The rugs and the drapes are gone. The pictures are gone. The floor is splintered and uneven. There are streaks and stains and blotches of mold on the plaster walls. The roof must have leaked.

A few tattered strips of wallpaper remain. Pink and blue flowers faded now to gray. Lily remembers helping Mama choose that pattern. She tightens her grip on the banister to keep herself from running back to the safety of the studio, where nothing has changed.

She looks down at the first floor. It's empty, ruined. The noisy men have torn it apart. Dust covers everything. The walls are open wood frameworks. She can see through them into every room.

The workmen are in the parlor. They lounge about, standing in corners, leaning against walls, eating buns and drinking coffee from paper cups. They wear their strange yellow hats and working clothes and heavy boots. One spits on the floor.

She stays in the shadows as she descends, stopping on every step to be certain nobody notices her. No one does.

Lily tiptoes past the parlor. She should be in plain sight, but the men continue talking and laughing as if she isn't there. One man looks right at her, and she can tell he doesn't see her. It's most peculiar.

Moving into a patch of bright sunlight, she stretches out her hand and looks for its shadow. It's not there. She lifts her foot. It casts no shadow either.

She remembers trying to see herself in the mirror on the wardrobe door, how blurred and indistinct she was, more of a mist than a reflection. She'd wondered then if people could see her. Now she's sure they can't. Jules and Maisie won't see her, even with their eyes wide open.

Invisibility gives Lily courage. If she can't be seen, she can't be hurt. She walks right past a man and glides into the kitchen. It's stripped bare, like the rest of the house. Aunt Nellie's stove is gone, her sink too. The shelves have disappeared, along with all the pots and pans.

She notices a new door. It must lead to the addition. She turns the knob, but it's locked. Through it, she hears voices. She smells bacon and remembers its smoky taste. Something in the empty place inside her aches.

She looks out a window and sees a path that leads to the meadow where Papa kept his dairy cows.

Summoning courage she didn't know she had, Lily slips outside through the open kitchen door. If no one can see her, she can go anywhere.

The sun hurts her eyes, and she stumbles, half blind. She doesn't remember how painfully bright sunlight is. She stands still and opens her eyes slowly. At first, she can't see anything but blobs of dark and light. Gradually her eyes stop hurting and her vision clears.

Her surroundings are familiar yet unfamiliar. Most of the trees are gone. What was once a green lawn is now a churned-up field of red mud. Nettles, milkweed, and Queen Anne's lace flourish where Mama's roses grew.

She walks farther from the house. Nothing is left of the barn except its stone foundation. Weeds and brambles grow in the pasture. Honeysuckle smothers sagging fences and broken stone walls.

No hens peck in the dirt. No rooster struts and crows. No cows rest in the grass. No sheep graze in the upper meadow. No corn rustles in the breeze, no wheat rippling like waves. No one works in the fields.

A blight has fallen on the farm.

Once more, Lily is tempted to run back to Papa's

studio and hide in the wardrobe, but in spite of the farm's desolation, the sky is blue and the sun is warm. It's good to be away from dust and dead insects and musty air. It's good to hear birds instead of hammers and saws and men shouting.

At last Lily comes to the field and sees the willow tree. It's much taller than she remembers. She's not even sure it's the same tree. Another might have grown in its place.

Except for the size of the willow, the field looks exactly the same as it did the day she and Papa and Mama had their last picnic by the stream. Wildflowers sway in a breeze. Birds sing. The sky arches overhead, a lovely shade of pure blue— the same blue as Papa's eyes.

A terrible loneliness casts a dark shadow over Lily. She's by herself in this spot where she was happy with Mama and Papa. Nothing has changed. Everything has changed.

Just as she's about to return to the house, Lily hears voices. Jules and Maisie are coming across the field.

Lily hesitates. Half of her longs to be seen. The other half is terrified of being seen. She smooths her ragged nightgown. She touches her hair. It's wild and tangled, unwashed, uncombed, unbrushed. It's grown very long. In truth, it almost touches the ground.

Mama would have a conniption fit if she saw Lily

outdoors in her nightgown, her hair uncombed and her feet bare.

She decides to hide in the willow tree and watch the girls from above. Silently she climbs from branch to branch, higher and higher. At some point she realizes that she isn't actually climbing. She no longer needs to hold on to the limbs of the willow. She lets a breeze carry her to the top of the tree and she perches there. The branches rock her gently.

This must be what it's like to be a bird. If only she had wings. She'd fly high into the sky and look down at the earth. Oh, what sights she'd see.

Lily watches Jules and Maisie brush aside the willow's drooping branches. They sit by the stream and dangle their bare feet in the water.

How small the girls are. How fragile. It breaks her heart to hear them talk and laugh. They do not know what Lily knows. She hopes they never will.

25

Jules

Maisie and I sat under the willow and waited for Lily. The sun splashed the ground with light and shadows. A dragonfly skimmed over the water.

"Do you think she'll really come?" Maisie asked.

"She *promised*."

A breeze riffled the leaves of the willow, and someone laughed. Maisie and I looked up. Sunlight flared in my eyes. I saw nothing but the tree.

"Lily?" I cried. "Is it you? Are you here?"

The willow leaves moved in one place, but the tree was motionless everywhere else.

"Please, Lily," Maisie called, "let us see you."

The willow swayed. Something light and small moved slowly from branch to branch, but I saw nothing except fluttering leaves.

Willing myself to see her, I closed my eyes, opened them, widened them, narrowed them, blinked, and blinked again.

Lily laughed. "I see you, but you can't see me. I'm invisible."

Her voice was right in front of us now. Squeezing my eyes shut again, I pictured the girl I'd glimpsed in the field, the one in the portrait — long blond hair, blue dress, ribbons in her hair. I pressed my eyelids shut until I saw flashes of light. Then slowly, slowly, I opened them, taking care not to look directly at the place where I guessed she'd be.

And there she was, sitting in the willow tree just above Maisie and me. She wore the dress I'd seen before, and her long, yellow hair was held back from her face with blue ribbons.

"Oh, Lily," I whispered. "You look exactly like you did the first time I saw you."

Maisie smiled. "You might have stepped right out of your father's painting — just as we wished you would."

26

Lily

Lily looks down at herself. Instead of a blue dress, she's wearing her disgraceful nightgown, yellow with age and worn almost transparent.

She tries to smooth her hair back from her face, but it's like pushing cobweb strands away. What she needs is a hot bath and a change of clothes. A pair of shoes would also be nice.

But perhaps it doesn't matter. Jules and Maisie see her as she once was, not as she is now.

Sitting quietly in the tree, she watches Papa's gerry bugs parade across the water's surface, tracing their ever-changing patterns of circles, over and over again. Above her head, leaves murmur like children telling secrets.

A bumblebee burrows into a flower. It's so easy to hide, she thinks, and so hard to be found.

"We're happy you came," Jules says. "We were worried you'd be scared to leave your room."

"I *was* afraid," Lily admits. "I've been there ever so long. I went downstairs, and I saw what's become of our house. It's in ruins. Everything we had is gone. The lawn is mud, Mama's garden is overgrown with weeds—the barns and sheds, the chickens, the cows . . . What have they done with it all?"

"Your house was empty for a long, long time," Maisie says.

"This big company hired my father to restore Oak Hill," Jules says. "When he's done, it will look almost like it did when you lived there."

Lily ponders what they have told her. "Please don't think I'm foolish, but when you say a long, long time, I don't know what you mean exactly. When I lived in Oak Hill— my real life with Mama and Papa and Aunt Nellie—it was 1889. What year is it now?"

The girls look at each other, as if they're afraid she won't like the answer to her question.

When Jules tells her, Lily feels as if she's been swallowed up by time. No one from her world is alive now. No one. Not even Mrs. Brown's new baby that was baptized the Sunday before everything changed.

When she can speak again, Lily says, "Reverend Donaldson told us the world would end in the year two thousand. Judgment Day would come, and the dead would rise from their graves, and we'd be sent to heaven or hell."

"In 1999, a lot of people thought the same thing," Maisie says. "They stocked up on food and water and prepared for the end of the world, but on the first day of two thousand, everything was just the same." She shrugged. "And here we are."

Yes, Lily thinks, here we are, but unlike Maisie and Jules, she doesn't belong in the twenty-first century. She belongs in 1889.

"I was born on the ninth of February in 1880," Lily says. "So I'm old now. Impossibly old."

Jules and Maisie nod.

No one is meant to live this long, Lily thinks. She should be dead, really and completely dead. She belongs in her grave, not sitting in a willow tree wearing a tattered nightgown and talking to living, breathing girls.

She looks at them. "I'm not supposed to be here, am I?"

The girls look at each other, their faces solemn. Lily senses that they have something to tell her. She sits quietly and waits for them to speak.

27

Jules

It seemed to me that Lily was thinking along the same lines as Maisie and I. She already knew she was in the wrong time. If we convinced her about alternate worlds, perhaps she'd do what had to be done to set things right.

"Maisie and I've been thinking about the night Mr. Bailey and Ellis Dixon came to your house," I told her. "What if you hadn't hidden upstairs? What would have happened?"

"But Mama told me to hide," Lily said. "I'd never disobey her or Papa."

"But suppose you knew what was going to happen," Maisie said. "Would you still obey your mother?"

Lily frowned and slowly shook her head. "I'd run downstairs after her. When the men came, they'd kill us all."

"That's not a very happy ending," I said.

Lily shrugged. "Don't you see? All I want is to be with

Mama and Papa. Even if we're dead, I'd be happier with them than I am without them."

"Think, Lily," I said. "Could you possibly have gotten help? What if you'd fetched the sheriff? Or a neighbor?"

"They were too far away," Lily said.

"How about the woman with the horses?" I asked. "Would she help you?"

"Aunt Nellie," Lily whispered. "Of course. She was outside with the horses that night. She'd *never* let anyone hurt me. She loved me as if I were her own child. Mama told me so."

"But she's Mr. Bailey's wife," Maisie said. "Would she go against her own husband?"

"Mr. Bailey's a bad man," Lily said. "He drinks whiskey and he hits Aunt Nellie and he stole Papa's money. She'd do anything to save me, even if he told her not to. So help me, if I had a gun, I'd shoot Mr. Bailey dead." She was so angry, her body quivered as if she might break into thousands of pieces and disappear. "I know about guns. Papa gave me lessons."

Maisie and I looked at each other in surprise. Lily was fiercer than she looked. With a temper like that, she might be brave enough to save her parents and herself.

Deciding this was the right moment to explain our

plan, I took a deep breath and said, "I'm going to tell you something you might not understand. In fact, you might not believe it. You might even think I've lost my mind."

When I paused, Maisie said, "Go on, tell her."

"Okay. Suppose this world isn't the only world. Suppose there are lots of other worlds, some almost like this one and others completely different."

"Mars, Venus, Saturn, Jupiter. I learned about them in school. Nobody lives on them. Except maybe Mars."

"I'm not talking about planets," I told her. "I mean worlds that astronomers can't see. They don't show up in telescopes. They exist in another dimension."

From the way Lily looked at me, I guessed she no longer understood what I meant. At this point I wasn't even sure I understood. It sounded too complicated to be true.

I tried again, hoping to convince myself as well as Lily. "It's not easy to explain, but things can happen in one world that don't happen in another world."

"Imagine there's a world where Mr. Bailey didn't kill anyone," Maisie said. "In that world, you and your parents are alive and happy."

"Do you mean heaven?" Lily asked.

"No, not heaven," Maisie said. "Please just be quiet and let us explain. It's really important, Lily."

"I'm sorry. I didn't mean to be rude." Lily folded her hands in her lap and sat up straight.

"It's all right. You weren't rude," I said. "It's hard to understand."

"Just tell her what to do," Maisie said.

"Are you brave, Lily?" I asked.

"I'm as brave as I can be," she said. "I'm not scared of snakes or thunder and lightning. I'm not even afraid of Papa's bull or Mr. Mason's hunting dogs."

"Are you brave enough to run outside tonight when the horsemen come? Are you brave enough to fetch Aunt Nellie?"

She hesitated. "Will you and Maisie be there?"

"Yes," we said together.

"All right then," Lily said. "I'll do it. I'll fetch Aunt Nellie. I'll be with Mama and Papa no matter what happens."

I looked at the child sitting above me in the tree and knew I'd never meet anyone, living or dead, as brave as Lily.

28

Lily

For a moment the two girls say nothing, and Lily is free to drift on the stream of memories time has returned to her. She looks across the field to the woods. The trees hide something in their shadows, something she should see. She can't quite remember what it is, but she doesn't want to be alone when she finds it.

Perhaps Jules and Maisie will come with her. She leans down from her branch, still worried that they might smell her dirty feet, and whispers, "Will you walk in the woods with me? It's cooler there."

"Of course," Jules says. She and Maisie scramble to their feet, and Lily drops down from the tree. She lands without a sound and leads the girls down a narrow path. It's so over-grown with weeds, Lily wouldn't have seen it if she hadn't known it was there.

Somewhere ahead, mourning doves coo, but she doesn't realize where she is until she sees the tombstones hidden in the deep shade. Weeds and ivy cling to them. Trees have grown up around them. The stones tilt and slant. Some have fallen. The graveyard looks very different from the last time Lily saw it.

Jules and Maisie stop. They both look frightened. Have they never seen a graveyard?

"Why have you brought us here?" Jules asks.

"You'll see." Lily drifts ahead of them. Her feet barely touch the ground.

She looks back at the girls. Maisie is making an effort to find a way through the weeds and brambles, but Jules hasn't moved. Is she scared of the dead?

Lily floats ahead. The grave closest to the path belongs to Grandfather and Grandmother Pettifer. Grandfather died before Lily was born, but she remembers Grandmother. Very old she was, wrinkled and worn, like clothing packed away too long at the bottom of a trunk. When her fingers clasped Lily's wrist, she felt as if she'd been caught by a bird with long talons.

Grandmother died when Lily was seven years old. Lily had stood where she is standing now, holding her parents' hands and watching the coffin disappear into the earth.

She'd cried, as much out of fright as of sorrow, for it was dreadful to think of Grandmother in that coffin, her sharp eyes closed forever.

Mama cried too, for the old woman was her mother and she'd loved her. Papa comforted both of them.

Lily walks farther into the graveyard. She looks under the ivy at the small headstones of Pettifer children who died when they were little and at the mossy stones where people older than memory are buried. Pettifer and a few other names appear over and over again. Her family is here, grandparents and great-grandparents, aunts, uncles, and cousins. All dead and buried properly.

At last she spies an angel hiding in the honeysuckle and wild grapevines. Its marble skin is mossy green from age and spotted with lichen and moss. Beautiful in grief, the angel kneels with drooping wings on a tomb. Lily has found what she seeks.

HERE LIE THE BODIES OF
HENRY BENNETT
and his wife, LAURA, *daughter of*
JAMES and SARAH PETTIFER
Struck down cruelly in the midst of life

And in Memory of their Beloved Daughter
Who was taken from us in her Childhood

LILIAN ANNE BENNETT

"Never more to find her where the bright waters flow . . .
Her smiles have vanished and her sweet songs flown."

Lily runs a finger over her parents' names: *Henry Bennett and his wife, Laura.* The letters are faded and blurred from years of snow and rain. Even though she knows that Papa and Mama are dead, it's something else altogether to stand here in the green shade and know they lie beneath the mossy earth at her feet.

She touches her own name. Does the inscription mean that she's buried with her parents, or does it mean that she's dead but not buried here? She thinks "in Memory" must mean she isn't here. No one found her. She hid too well.

When she reads what's written beneath her name, she smiles. The words are from a song Mama often sang to her. Lily is pleased to see its words on the tombstone.

"'I dream of Jeannie with the light brown hair . . .'" Lily sings in a sweet voice. Maisie and Jules sing with her. They stop after the first verse, but Lily remembers every word. She sings all the way to Jeannie's death at the song's ending.

Maisie stands beside her, and Jules stands on the other

side. It's a solemn moment, Lily thinks, like being in church. She wishes she were solid so she could hold their warm hands.

"If Mr. Bailey and Ellis Dixon had found me, I'd be buried here with Mama and Papa." Lily turns to the girls. She's frightened, she needs their comfort. In a whisper, she adds, "Maybe it's where I should be."

"No, Lily," Jules says. "*We* found you — Maisie and me. We'll make sure you go where you belong."

"To that other world," Maisie adds. "Where nobody dies at Oak Hill."

"I thought I was waiting for Mama and Papa," Lily says softly, "but maybe I was waiting for you all along."

"Tonight," Jules says, "everything will be the way it should be."

But Lily isn't listening. She fades silently into the dense shade and disappears. She needs to be alone. Invisible to everyone now, she curls up on the ground and lies still. Willing herself to sink into the earth, she longs to join her parents.

She hears the girls calling her, but she doesn't answer. She'll see them tonight. After a while they leave the cemetery. Their voices are so low she cannot hear what they say. She hopes she hasn't hurt their feelings or been rude.

Day slowly darkens into night. The air turns cold and damp. Nothing happens. Nothing changes. Slowly, she follows the narrow path to Oak Hill.

In the dark, the house looks the same as it did the night Papa carried her home from the picnic. She expects her parents to welcome her at the door, to ask where she's been, but she sees nothing except shadows, hears nothing but the night breeze blowing bits of trash across the floor.

Wearily she climbs the steps and enters Papa's studio. Mama and Papa are not there. Lily is alone.

29

Jules

I spun around and looked for Lily. "Where did she go?"

"Lily," Maisie called. "Lily!"

No one answered but a mourning dove hidden in the shade.

We called her name again and again. The mourning dove cooed its sad song over and over, but Lily didn't answer, and she didn't appear.

"Where are you?" I called. "Please come out where we can see you."

"She's hiding," Maisie said. "We won't find her unless she wants us to."

Maisie and I stood silently and waited. All around us the trees creaked and sighed, as if they were telling each other secrets. I thought of their roots tangled together under the earth, binding them together in the dark. They held the coffins as well, keeping the dead safe.

The mourning dove cooed, but Lily didn't return.

At exactly the same moment, Maisie and I reached out to touch Lily's name. Our fingers brushed against each other on the rough stone. Friends, we were friends, I knew without asking. Even if I moved to Alaska or Hawaii, Maisie and I would be friends because of Lily.

"We should clean up the graveyard," Maisie said. "It's wrong for Lily's family to lie here forgotten."

"If we tell Dad about it, maybe his work crew will do it."

"And after they finish the hard work, we can plant flowers and stuff for Lily," Maisie said.

"A memorial garden," I said, and she nodded.

Slowly we made our way out of the graveyard and followed the path uphill through the woods. In the damp shade, gnats swarmed around our heads and mosquitoes attacked us.

"Do you think our plan will really work?" I asked Maisie. Now that I knew Lily, I felt as if we were sending a real live child into terrible danger.

When Maisie didn't answer right away, I asked her another question. "Aren't you afraid Mr. Bailey will kill Lily?"

"It's so complicated." Maisie wiped the sweat from

her forehead. "There could be a world where Mr. Bennett didn't fire Mr. Bailey. There could be a world where he hired some other man. There could be a world where Mr. Bennett never met Lily's mother, and Lily was never born. There could be—"

I covered my ears. "Stop it! You're driving me insane."

"Sorry." Maisie squashed a mosquito on her arm. A bright bead of blood popped up and she smeared it away. "Wouldn't it be great to live in a world where nothing bit you?"

We walked on, swatting gnats and mosquitoes, our shirts soaked with sweat despite the shade.

From somewhere ahead I heard voices. "Your mother must be here. Do you think she'll let you stay tonight?"

Maisie turned to me, red-faced from the heat. "She has to. I'm not letting you go in that house alone."

"That's a relief!" I laughed as if it were no big thing, but for the first time, I knew what it was like to have a good friend. I felt like doing a row of cartwheels all the way home, but I wasn't very good at gymnastics. And besides that, it was way too hot to try.

When we came out of the woods, we saw our mothers sitting on the deck, talking like old friends.

Maisie's mom saw us first and waved for us to join her

and Mom on the deck. We collapsed on the picnic table, too hot and tired to take another step.

"How about a big glass of ice-cold lemonade?" Mom asked.

Maisie and I drank ours in about one minute, and Mom poured us seconds.

"Have you girls had fun?" Maisie's mom asked.

Maisie nodded and took another gulp of lemonade. "We've had a great time. Can I stay another night?"

"Of course," our mothers said in unison, and laughed at their unplanned duet.

The two of them went on with their conversation, and Maisie and I went inside to cool off in air-conditioned comfort. We had things to talk about and plans to make.

30

Jules

After dinner that night, we kept ourselves from think-ing about our plan by playing a few games of Clue with my parents. I won the first round by accusing Colonel Mustard of murdering Mr. Boddy in the library with a knife. Maisie won the second by accusing Mrs. White of killing Mr. Boddy in the kitchen with a wrench. Mom won the third game, and Maisie won the fourth.

"Poor Mr. Boddy," Dad said. "Always dead before the game even begins."

We started a fifth game, but Dad insisted that we use the British words. We had to call the wrench a *spanner* and the knife a *dirk*.

He also said that Mr. Boddy shouldn't always be the murder victim. "Give the poor man a break, and let that old bore Colonel Mustard be the one to die."

I was already having trouble paying attention to the game. With Dad making up new rules all the time, I was too distracted to keep playing.

I glanced at Maisie and caught her looking at the window, as if she expected to see the horsemen galloping toward Oak Hill.

"I'm so tired," I said. "How about you, Maisie?"

She yawned so widely the fillings in her back teeth showed.

"Oh, girls, for heaven's sake, go to bed before you fall asleep on the couch," Mom said. "We've played enough Clue for tonight."

"More than enough," Dad said. "It's time to bury poor departed Mr. Boddy." He dumped everything into the box and closed the lid. "Rest in peace, old boy."

I kissed him and Mom good night and left them arguing over what TV show to watch.

In my room, Maisie and I checked our flashlight batteries and settled down to wait for my parents to go to bed. After Dad began snoring, we tiptoed into the kitchen and opened the door to the old house. At the same moment, we heard the horses galloping toward us.

"Hurry," I whispered. "We've got to hide."

Darting into the old house, we flattened ourselves

against a wall near the stairs and stared about us in disbelief. Instead of the ruins we expected to see, Oak Hill looked as it must have when Lily lived here. The walls were papered, and the floor gleamed with polish. A kerosene lamp on a small marble-topped table lit a group of portraits—not of Lily and her parents but of people from even longer ago, Lily's ancestors probably, dark with age.

Upstairs, Lily whimpered, and Mrs. Bennett ran down the steps. As she passed us, her long skirt brushed against me, but she didn't notice me or Maisie. It seemed we were invisible witnesses to what was about to happen.

We watched Mrs. Bennett join her husband in the kitchen. Fists pounded on the kitchen door.

"Don't let them in," Mrs. Bennett cried.

But the men forced the door open and entered the kitchen, shouting and cursing.

Mr. Bennett faced the men, his back to us. Mrs. Bennett stood beside him. "Go home," he told them. "You have no business here!"

"I worked for you more than five years. You owe me more than a week's salary." Mr. Bailey was a big man, taller and heavier than Mr. Bennett, and just as ugly as he'd looked in Lily's drawings.

Ellis Dixon pushed his way forward. He looked like a

ferret, short and skinny, with a narrow face and close-set eyes. "Money," he said. "That's what we come for. Give us what's in your safe."

"You're a pair of drunken fools," Mr. Bennett said. "Get out of my house."

"Please," Mrs. Bennett said. "Leave now."

Mr. Bailey pointed a gun at Mr. Bennett. "Don't tell me what to do. I ain't your tenant no more. You listen to me now!"

At the same moment, Ellis Dixon twisted Mrs. Bennett's arm behind her back. "Take us to the safe and open it."

Flattening ourselves against the wall, Maisie and I watched the killers force the Bennetts past us and into the parlor. They were close enough for me to smell the whiskey on their breath and the sour odor of sweat and stale tobacco, but they didn't notice Maisie and me.

Mr. Bennett struggled to free himself, and Mrs. Bennett pleaded with the men to let them go.

We heard a faint noise overhead. Lily stood at the top of the steps. She wore a long white nightgown and her yellow hair hung in loose curls around her face.

For a moment it seemed as if she might turn and run back to the studio.

"Lily," I whispered, "we're here. Be brave."

She didn't seem to see us, but she gripped the banister and inched down the steps. She was pale with fear, but determined.

"Fetch Aunt Nellie. Change what happens," Maisie said.

Holding our breath, we watched Lily take one step down, then another. From the parlor, we heard Mr. Bailey shouting. Mr. Bennett shouted back. Mrs. Bennett sobbed softly.

Lily hesitated at the foot of the steps and looked toward the parlor.

"No, no," I whispered. "If you go in there, you won't save anyone. You'll all die."

She took a step toward the parlor. Her mother was still crying. Her father spoke angrily. The killers shouted about the safe and the money.

Lily was at the doorway now. She paid no attention to us. It was as if we didn't exist — in this world, maybe we didn't.

We had to stop her, but even when I grabbed her arm, she didn't react.

"Lily," we shouted. "Don't let them see you! Go outside. Get Aunt Nellie! Change what happens!"

Sill ignoring us, Lily listened at the door for a few seconds. Maisie and I shouted at her. She didn't hear us. And neither did anyone else.

Suddenly Lily cocked her head like a cat who's just noticed a mouse. She looked at Maisie and me, not exactly with recognition, and backed away from the doorway.

Outside in the dark, a horse whinnied. A woman spoke in a low voice.

"Go," we shouted to Lily, "get Aunt Nellie!"

Without looking at Maisie or me, Lily ran down the hall and into the kitchen. A moment later a door opened and a breath of cool night air stirred the window curtains.

31

Lily

From the top step, Lily watches her mother run downstairs. It's hard to disobey Mama, even though she has a very strong urge to do so. So instead of locking herself in the studio, she clings to the banister. Below her, Mama hurries to the kitchen. The men are in the house now. She hears them cursing Papa.

Mr. Bailey and Ellis Dixon come out of the kitchen and into the hall. With guns in their hands, they force Papa and Mama into the parlor. They want money. Papa's money.

Lily knows the safe is hidden behind one of Papa's paintings. Lily saw it once when Papa opened it to put in a box of money from crop sales. The men tell him to open the safe and give them the money. All of it.

Maybe Papa will give them the money and the men will leave and all will be well.

When Mama begins to cry, Lily creeps slowly and silently down the steps and tiptoes toward the parlor. While Mama weeps, Papa shouts at the men, and they shout back. The angry voices frighten Lily.

Mama and Papa are in danger. Lily must save them, but how is she to do that? Suddenly she's aware that someone or something is trying to tell her what to do. She looks around, but sees no one.

Outside in the dark, a horse whinnies and a woman speaks softly.

Lily knows she must get help, but she's too scared to move. She hears a voice and sees two girls crouching in the hall. They cry, "Don't let them see you, Lily! Go outside. Get Aunt Nellie! Change what happens!"

She doesn't know who they are or where they came from, but almost against her will she does what they tell her. Dashing out the back door, she calls to Aunt Nellie for help.

When she sees Lily, Aunt Nellie drops the reins and runs toward her. "Lily, Lily!" she calls.

Lily seizes Aunt Nellie's hands. "Don't let them hurt Mama and Papa! They have guns."

"Lord God Almighty!" Aunt Nellie cries. "He promised he'd not harm anyone."

Seizing Lily's hand, Aunt Nellie runs toward the house, but before she reaches the door, Mr. Bailey steps outside.

"What's gotten into you?" he shouts at his wife. "Put the girl down and mind them horses like I told you."

He steps toward them, his face like the devil's, ugly with anger and hate.

Lily sees his revolver. Too angry to be afraid, she pulls away from Aunt Nellie and hurls herself at Mr. Bailey. She'll make sure he doesn't hurt anyone.

The man grabs Lily and lifts her off her feet. He holds her under her arms as if she's a dog. His breath smokes with whiskey and his eyes are wicked, like the eyes of the old bull Papa keeps in the pasture.

Lily struggles, she kicks, she flails at him with her fists; she squirms and twists like a cat who doesn't want to be held. If only she had claws, she'd scratch his eyes out.

Her heart pounds with fear and rage, she can hardly breathe, but she's never felt so strong. She, Lily, will save Mama and Papa.

While Lily keeps Mr. Bailey busy, Aunt Nellie ducks around him and runs into the house.

Mr. Bailey follows her. "Get back outside," he shouts at his wife. "What happens in this house ain't no business of yours."

Lily kicks him and strikes him with her fists, but he manages to hold her with one arm and keep his gun pointed at his wife. All three of them join Mama and Papa in the parlor. Ellis Dixon keeps his gun pointed at Mama and Papa, but he looks startled to see Lily.

"What the devil's going on?" he asks. "Where'd the girl come from?"

At the same moment, Mama cries, "For the Lord's sake, put my daughter down. Don't hurt her!"

Papa lunges toward Mr. Bailey. "Let Lily go!"

Lily takes advantage of the confusion. She might not have claws, but she has teeth. With savage ferocity, she sinks them into the hand that holds the gun. She tastes blood.

Taken by surprise, Mr. Bailey drops the gun and loosens his grip on Lily. With a burst of strength, she squirms free and runs to Mama just as Aunt Nellie picks up the pistol and points it at Mr. Bailey.

Mama holds Lily so tightly she can hardly breathe. She kisses Lily's hair, her face, her hands. She murmurs and sighs and starts to cry. "Oh, Lily, Lily, Lily," she whispers.

"Stop right now, Charlie," Aunt Nellie says, "or I'll shoot you dead. Don't think I won't. There ain't a soul in this world who'd blame me."

Lily peeks across the room. Aunt Nellie is aiming the gun right at Mr. Bailey. She looks angry enough to pull the trigger.

"Give me that gun, Nellie." Mr. Bailey holds out his hand. "You won't shoot me. You ain't got the stomach for it."

Aunt Nellie keeps the gun aimed at him. "I'll blow your head off. You been asking for it since the first time you hit me."

Lily hopes that Aunt Nellie will shoot Mr. Bailey soon. If she won't, Lily will grab the gun and kill him herself. Her fingers itch to pull the trigger. She hates him, she wants him dead, dead, dead. She must be the baddest girl in the world, but she doesn't care.

Ellis Dixon stands near Papa. His gun's muzzle touches Papa's head. He looks stunned, as if he's forgotten why he's in the parlor or what a gun is for.

"What are you waiting for?" Mr. Bailey shouts. "Shoot her if you have to. Just get the gun, Ellis."

Lily can't keep up with what happens next. First she hears a gunshot so loud it makes her ears ring. Next she sees Mr. Bailey fall to the floor. His head is bleeding. A red stain spreads across the carpet.

Lily trembles and presses her face against Mama's

shoulder. Even though she's just wished him dead, she doesn't want to see his blood. Her fierceness melts away. She clings to Mama like a baby.

Mama murmurs, "It's all right, Lily. We're safe now."

"Did she shoot him dead?" Lily whispers, afraid to look and see for herself.

"Ellis shot him." Papa drops to his knees beside Mr. Bailey and feels for a pulse. "I believe he's dead."

Ellis Dixon moans and cries. "It's your fault, Bennett. You grabbed my arm. I was aiming at that woman, but I shot Charlie instead."

Pushing Papa aside, he kneels beside Mr. Bailey. "Oh, Charlie, forgive me, I never meant to do it."

Lily lifts her head just in time to see Papa drag Ellis Dixon to a chair and tie his arms and feet with cords from the drapes.

She expects Ellis Dixon to put up a fight, but he just sits there and lets Papa knot the rope good and tight. His face is as white as a dead man's and he's shaking all over.

"Oh, Lord, what have I done?" he groans. "What have I done?"

Aunt Nellie still has her husband's gun. She's sitting down now, so it's cradled in her lap. "I never would have shot him," she mutters. "He was right, I don't have the stomach for such things. But Lord, I'm glad Dixon killed him. I won't miss that man. No indeed."

Mr. Bailey lies on the floor where he fell. Mama covers him with one of her good linen tablecloths. Lily is sure his blood will never wash out of it.

"Mama," she whispers. "Mama, I was scared. I thought they'd kill us all."

"Oh, Lily, I was scared too." Mama hugs her, and Papa embraces them both.

"Thank the Lord, we're all safe." He sounds close to tears.

"How long will Mr. Bailey be lying there? And how long will Ellis Dixon be tied to the chair?" Lily asks. She wants everything to be cleaned up. No reminders of what happened here.

"I'll fetch the sheriff tomorrow," Papa says. "He'll take Dixon to jail and remove Mr. Bailey's body."

Papa turns to Mama. "Perhaps you should take Lily to bed," he says. "This has been a terrible night for all of us."

Lily clings to Papa for a moment. "Don't ever leave me," she begs. She isn't sure why, but she has a strange feeling he might have left her once.

He kisses Lily's tears away. "Don't worry, dearest. I'll never leave you."

"And neither will you, Mama?"

"Never, never, never." Mama gives Lily a kiss for each *never*.

As Mama carries her up the stairs, Lily looks over the banister. For a moment she sees the same two girls looking up at her from the shadows. Or are they ghosts? When they wave to her, she waves back.

"Who did you wave to?" Mama asks.

Lily points at the girls, but they aren't there anymore. She rests her head on Mama's shoulder and closes her eyes. "Nobody," she whispers.

Mama lays Lily on her bed. Her favorite china doll sprawls on its face on the floor. Mama picks it up. "Oh, no. Her head is cracked. She must have fallen off the bed when I woke you."

Lily reaches for the doll. "Can you fix her?"

"Papa's very good at mending china. He'll make her look almost as good as new."

Lilly rocks the doll gently. "I was worried that you might throw her in the midden with the trash."

"Of course not. Whatever gave you that notion?"

Lily has no idea where that notion came from. Mama wouldn't throw her doll away. Yet she's sure she saw the doll in the midden, bald and falling to pieces and ugly. She's glad it's not true. Papa will mend the cracks, and the doll will be almost as pretty as the day Grandmother Pettifer gave it to her.

She lies back on her pillow and clasps her mother's hand. "I hope you aren't cross with me for disobeying you."

Mama squeezes Lily's hands. "If you hadn't fetched Nellie, things might have gone very badly for us." Mama lies down beside her. "Close your eyes and sleep now."

"Will you sing 'Jeannie with the Light Brown Hair'?"

"Of course I will."

Lily falls asleep listening to Mama's soft voice. She's safe now; she's where she belongs.

32

Jules

W'd watched the scene in the parlor as if it were the last act of a play seen in dim light through a dingy curtain. The actors were barely visible, their voices almost inaudible, and the plot was hard to follow, but it had the ending we'd hoped for.

Now the play was over, and we were alone in the dark. Lily was gone. Oak Hill was in ruins again. Moonlight slanted through the windows of the old house and shone on piles of rubbish and the plywood subflooring and the skeletal wooden framework of the walls. Tools and extension cords, ladders and brooms, paper cups, empty paper bags, and soda cans lay where the workmen had left them.

"Lily did it," Maisie said. "She saved her parents and herself."

"I could never be as brave as she was."

"Me neither," Maisie said. "I was worried at first, though, weren't you?"

"You mean when she just stood there like she was frozen or something?"

"And we kept shouting and she couldn't hear us. . . ."

"It was like we were the ghosts instead of Lily."

We sat for a while and listened to the old house. Except for occasional creaks, it was silent. Empty. Lily wasn't hiding in the room on the third floor. I'd never glimpse her at the window again, I'd never hear the horsemen. Their fates were settled.

Maisie yawned and looked at her watch. "It's after four a.m."

We brushed sawdust off our pajama pants and let ourselves into the addition. The Clue game lay on the table where we'd left it. Our ice-cream bowls sat in the sink, rinsed but not washed. The kitchen clock ticked, and the night-light cast a dim glow on the stove-top.

Moonlight dappled the field behind the house, and the woods lay in darkness. Two deer, followed by a fawn, leaped through the tall weeds and vanished into the trees. On the Interstate, trucks rumbled.

To everyone but Maisie and me, it was an ordinary night.

33

Jules

The next morning, we slept so late that Mom checked to make sure we were breathing. "You girls would sleep all day if I let you." Feeling groggy, we dressed and ate breakfast.

Leaving Mom at work on her novel, we walked down to the willow tree.

"Last night is so hard to believe," Maisie said.

I tossed a pebble into the stream and watched its rings spread across the water. "If you hadn't been there, I'd think it was a dream."

"It seems that way now." Maisie threw a pebble after mine. "Who'd ever believe something like that could actually happen?"

A breeze rustled the leaves overhead. We squinted at the

sun flashing down through the willow leaves, but this time nothing stirred in the branches. "She's not there, is she?"

"No."

I watched the Gerridae waltz across the water. Beneath them, minnows darted about, turning this way and that in unison. Birds sang, bees buzzed in the clover, and a rabbit studied us from the edge of a bramble patch. It was just like the day before, but because of Lily, everything had changed.

Maisie sat beside me, making a chain of clover blossoms. "Was Lily really in our world?" I asked. "Or was she stuck between two worlds, neither in one or the other, until she disobeyed her mother and went downstairs to save her family?"

Maisie frowned and ran a hand through her hair. "It's just so complicated," she finally said. "In one world, Lily and her parents die, but in another world, she and her parents live."

"Our world must be the world she died in," I said softly. "That's why Oak Hill is in ruins."

"If that's true," Maisie said, "the dolls we found in the midden will be where we left them."

Between the heat and the gnats circling my head, my

brain felt as mushy as a watermelon. Suddenly I was too irritated to think about anything more complicated than one plus one. "I don't know, Maisie. I don't know, I just do not know!"

"You needn't shout," Maisie said. "I'm not deaf, you know." She stood up and started walking toward the house.

Afraid she was mad at me, I ran after her. "Where are you going?"

"To the midden," Maisie said, "to see if the dolls are there."

Without another word we headed across the field and up the hill. Yesterday we'd left the doll and her small companions on the grass by the hole I'd dug. In the excitement of last night, we'd forgotten all about them.

As soon as we came out of the woods, we saw the little china dolls lying on their backs in a row next to the bald doll—just exactly as we'd left them. Except for Lily's absence, nothing had changed.

Maisie knelt in the weeds and touched each doll as if it were a sacred relic from the past. "These belonged to Lily. She's gone, but they're still here."

I stared at the little dolls with some distrust—once, I thought they'd spoken out loud to me, but I must have imagined that. Today they were simply little china figurines, incapable of speech or movement. I turned away from the bald doll. She looked like a corpse dug up from her grave.

"Lily loved that doll," Maisie whispered. "She never would have thrown it in the midden."

"Mr. Bailey and Ellis Dixon probably did it," I said. "They looted the house and left the stuff they didn't want here in the dirt."

From where we knelt by the midden, we heard the noise of hammers and saws coming from the third floor. I looked up as one of the men opened the window in Lily's room.

"Hey, you two," he called down to us. "What are you doing in the trash heap? Go play somewhere safe. You could cut yourself on something."

Gathering the dolls, we ran around the corner of the house. Maisie's mother's car was parked by the back door. Inside, we found her, Mom, and Dad gathered around the kitchen table. Stacked up against one wall were the paintings from Henry Bennett's studio.

"Look what I found on the third floor." Dad pointed at the paintings. "Remember Henry Bennett? This is his work. Isn't it beautiful?"

The bright light of the kitchen lit the colors and details. Portraits and landscapes sprang to life. Maisie and I oohed and aahed, as if we'd never seen them.

"Just look at this one." Dad pulled out the portrait of Lily sitting in the willow tree. "Have you ever seen a more lifelike painting? You almost expect her to jump out of the tree and talk to you."

"Of all of them, it's my favorite," Mom said.

"Such a dear little face," Mrs. Sullivan said. "I wonder who she was."

"I'd guess she's Bennett's daughter, Lily." Dad showed Mrs. Sullivan another painting. "This is his wife, Laura. And here's one that shows Oak Hill as it was when the Bennetts lived here."

"What are you going to do with them?" she asked.

"The Taubman Museum in Roanoke already owns a small collection of Bennett's work," Mom said. "They're bound to be interested."

Dad sighed. "Stonybrook owns the paintings, but I'm sure the corporation will donate most of them to the Taubman or some other museum—another tax write-off for them, as well as a gift for the public."

I pointed to the picture of Lily in the tree. "Is there any way we could keep this one?"

"I'll ask." Dad laughed. "Maybe the corporation will give me one as a bonus for finding them."

Mom set two tall glasses of iced tea in front of Maisie

and me. "You two have been out in the heat too long. Red faces, red noses. I bet you forgot to use sun shield."

While we gulped our tea, Mom picked up the bald doll. "Where on earth did you find this poor thing?"

"In the midden," I told her. "We think she belonged to Lily."

"Yes," Mom murmured. "This must be the doll in several of the paintings."

"Can she be fixed up to look like she used to?" Maisie asked.

Mom sighed. "She's pretty far gone, but I once knew a woman who did wonders with antique dolls. Maybe I'll send her this poor lost soul and see what she can do."

"We found these, too." Maisie and I pulled the little dolls from our pockets and laid them on the kitchen counter.

"Frozen Charlottes." Mom smiled in recognition. "I had one or two when I was little, but I don't know what happened to them. They belonged to my grandmother."

"Why are they called Frozen Charlottes?" Maisie asked.

"They were named after a girl in an old song who froze to death because she was too vain to hide her party dress under an old cloak. Her mother warned her, but—"

"Nice story," Dad said as he picked up the smallest doll. "I thought they were called that because their arms and legs don't move."

Turning to us, he said, "Have you young detectives discovered anything else?"

"There's a family graveyard in the woods," Maisie told him. "It's almost hidden under vines and briars and weeds."

"Can you tell your workmen to clean it up?" I asked.

"It's definitely of historic value," Maisie said.

"Oh, will you show it to me?" Mom asked. "I love old burial grounds."

"I'd like to see it too," Maisie's mother said.

"Let's take a look after lunch," Dad suggested. "I'm sure the graveyard will be included in the restoration plans."

I had to ask one more thing, even though I was scared to hear the answer. "Was there anything in the room besides Henry Bennett's paintings?"

"His easel, some odds and ends of furniture, a big wardrobe."

"Did you look inside the wardrobe?" I glanced at Maisie and saw her eyes widen. She knew why I was asking.

"We pulled everything out in case he'd stashed more paintings inside, but all we found were rags—women's dresses mostly. They probably belonged to his wife."

Maisie and I sighed so loudly that Dad laughed. "What were you expecting? Skeletons in the closet?"

I forced myself to laugh, and Maisie joined in. "No, of course not," I said. "Books maybe, more paintings. I don't know. Just curious."

Maisie's mother stood up. "Now, if you girls will excuse us," she said, "we have some important matters to discuss."

For the first time, I noticed plans and official forms laid out on the kitchen counter.

"What's going on?" I asked Dad. "Are you already planning our next move?"

"I hope not," Mrs. Sullivan said. "My husband and I are on the town council. We've gotten funding for a project to restore the old buildings on Main Street. We're hoping to hire your father to take charge of the renovation work."

"You mean we'll stay here in Hillsborough?" I stared at him, not daring to believe what I was hearing.

"That would be the plan, yes," Dad told me. "Of course, if you'd rather move across the country, I'll tell the Sullivans I can't do it."

I ran around the table to hug him. "Say yes, Dad, say yes!"

Maisie chimed in. "Please, Mr. Aldridge, say yes!"

"Well, now, maybe your mother —"

"Don't be an idiot, Ron. Of course I want to stay in Hillsborough."

Dad spread his arms in a gesture of defeat. "It looks like my roaming days are over—at least for now."

I was too excited to sit still. Grabbing Maisie's hand, I ran outside and began turning cartwheels in the grass. For once, I didn't care what I looked like doing them.

Maisie followed me and collapsed when I did. "Your cartwheels are even worse than mine," she said.

We lay on our backs and laughed. Nothing was funny. Everything was funny.

✦

That evening, while Mom and Dad washed the dinner dishes, I sat on the deck and watched the stars come out. Just the evening star at first, then a few more, and then too many to count. A sliver of moon swung into sight over the mountains.

My thoughts strayed to Lily. I wished I could see her once more. Just once. I needed to know that Maisie's and my plan had worked, and she was safe.

I stared at the field where I'd first seen her with her parents. Would it be possible to see her there again? I concentrated all my mental energy on Lily, willing her to appear. "Only for a moment," I breathed, "that's all."

No luck this time. In the kitchen, Mom laughed at

something Dad said. Out of sight, traffic rumbled like waves pounding the shore. The cicadas made their usual racket in the woods.

The past had closed in on itself. Lily was safe in her world, and I was safe in mine. Most important now, Maisie and I had become friends. We'd be together all summer, and when school started, I wouldn't be alone.

More chills and thrills by

MARY DOWNING HAHN

A CHANGELING TALE

1

I WAS IN A TEMPER fit to blow the lid off a kettle of boiling water. And who wouldn't be? Since sunup, I'd been doing chores. I'd milked the cow, hauled two buckets of water from the well, fed the chickens, and then fought the hens for their eggs. Now I was down on my knees, sweat-soaked and bug-bitten, yanking weeds from the vegetable patch. My hands were caked with mud, and my nose was burned as red as a strawberry. Midges hummed around my face and bit my ears.

Wiping the sweat from my eyes, I yanked a thistle out by its roots, only to see two more hiding in the beans. I scowled at my baby brother, Thomas, who lay nearby on the grass.

"You," I muttered. "If it weren't for you, I'd be down the lane, skipping rope with the village girls. But, oh no, I must watch you and do chores as if I were a servant. You've ruined my life, that's what you've done. It's a wicked thing to say, but sometimes I wish you'd never been born!"

Thomas smiled at me and cooed as if I'd praised him. Ashamed, I clapped my hand over my mouth and hoped Mam hadn't heard me, but she was in the cottage, singing at her loom, weaving soft blankets to keep Thomas warm when winter came.

I watched Thomas playing with his toes and chuckling to himself. Truth to tell, he was a sweet baby, I'd be lying if I said he wasn't. He never fussed, never cried, he ate what he was fed, and slept the whole night through.

And he was beautiful, even though no one said so. When visitors came, they leaned over the cradle and frowned and scowled and shook their heads.

"'Tis a pity he's so ugly and puny," they'd say.

"Oh, yes, he's a sickly one. He'll not live past his first year."

"And such a nasty temper he's got."

"No good will come of him."

"If I caught a fish half as ugly as that poor babby, I'd throw it back."

It was as if each visitor tried to come up with a worse insult than the one before.

And all the while, Mam and Dadoe and I smiled and nodded in agreement, for all of us, even the youngest, knew it was bad luck to compliment a baby. Since the day my brother was born, I'd been warned not to speak of his pretty curls or his blue eyes or his dimples. I mustn't boast of his sweet nature or praise him in any way.

It was the Kinde Folke we feared. Although no one in our village had seen them for many a year, they could be far away or just outside the cottage door. They were sly and full of tricks, and no matter what we called them, they were far from kind, though no one ever dared say that aloud either. If we spoke of them at all, it was to say they were wise, they were beautiful, they were brave and noble and honest in their dealings.

When in truth, if we offended them, they burned our barns and cottages, stole our livestock, sent plagues to sicken us, cursed our fields with thistles, lamed our horses, and dried up our cows' milk.

Worst of all, if the Kinde Folke learned of a beautiful baby boy's birth, they'd steal him away and leave one of their own sickly creatures in his place. And what misery the changeling would bring to its new mother. As if it weren't bad enough that her own sweet baby was gone, changelings screamed and cried and bit and pinched and broke things. She'd have no rest, that poor mother, no joy.

And so we did our best to keep Thomas safe. I watched him while Mam did her housework, and she and Dadoe watched him at night. We never even whispered sweet things to him for fear the Kinde Folke would come for him.

Their spies were everywhere. Long-eared rabbits listened in the hedges, and sharp-eyed crows watched from chimney tops. Toads in ponds, fish in streams, foxes slinking by, any and all might carry messages to the Kinde Folke.

I stabbed my trowel into the dirt and dug out a stubborn thistle. I shouldn't have spoken so crossly to Thomas. He was too young to understand my words, but he must have heard the anger in my voice.

A crow cawed, and I looked up to see him perched in a tree over my head. He ruffled his black wings and stared down at me. His dark eye reflected a sliver of light. Keeping watch on me, he cawed again. It sounded as if he were laughing at me.

Suddenly anxious, I glanced at Thomas. He'd just learned to sit up, and he was looking at me to make sure I'd noticed. The small chain he always wore around his neck lay in the grass. Its silver locket sparkled in the sunlight.

Dropping the trowel, I ran to fetch the locket. "Old Granny Hedgepath gave you this, Thomas. You're not to take it off.

You'd best do what that old witch says, or she'll eat you for dinner."

Thomas laughed and clapped his hands. What did he know of witches and their ways?

I tried to slip the necklace over his head, but he grabbed the chain and held it out for me to take. Giving things to people was his new game. Most people, including me, gave them back, but Matthew down the lane had run home with the wooden cow Dadoe had carved for Thomas. I'd gone to his house and asked him for it.

"Babby give it me," Matthew wailed. Luckily for Thomas, but not for Matthew, his mam snatched the toy cow, handed it to me, and gave Matthew a smack.

I took the chain from Thomas and smiled. Without thinking, I said, "Oh, Thomas, you're so sweet. How could I ever be vexed with you? You're the best baby in the world. And the prettiest."

When I tried again to slip the chain over his head, he ducked away laughing.

I held the necklace out, but instead of continuing the struggle, I sat in the grass and admired the necklace. The silver chain was finely made, and the heart-shaped locket was decorated all over with a cunning pattern of vines and flowers. I sighed. It was much too pretty to waste on a boy.

In truth, I'd wanted the locket from the day Granny Hedgepath fastened the chain around my brother's neck. "Make sure Thomas wears this always," she'd told Mam. "Never remove it. He must eat and sleep with it around his neck. Even when you bathe him, make sure the locket stays fastened. It will protect him from mischief."

Placing her bony hand on Thomas's head, Granny added, "May the Kinde Folke of the forest find joy elsewhere and ignore this poor ugly baby."

I was watching Granny from my shadowy corner, neither moving nor speaking. It frightened me to look at her, but she drew my eyes like the evil cockatrice. Her white hair was wild and uncombed. Sticks and leaves poked out of its tangles. She had long yellow fingernails, as sharp as a hawk's talons, and her eyes were sunken so deep in their sockets, I couldn't tell their color.

Some said the old woman was a healer, others said she was witch, but everyone in the village agreed she knew magic and spells and walked in Mirkwood at midnight. They also knew not to anger her.

Suddenly Granny turned to me in my corner. "Why are you sulking there, girl? I see your sly eyes, I hear the beat of your jealous heart. The necklace is for your brother. You have no need for it."

She spoke as if I were a wicked girl, a bad sister, someone not to be trusted. Even though it was rude, I turned my head away and scowled at the floor. How had Granny guessed I wanted that necklace? It belonged around my neck, not my brother's.

After Granny left, Mam said, "You shamed me, Mollie. I've taught you to smile and curtsy when you see Granny Hedgepath, but you did neither. What must she think of you?"

"I don't care what she thinks. Did you not hear what she said to me? She was hateful and rude."

"No, it was you who was hateful and rude." Mam looked at me. "I hope you haven't made an enemy of that old woman."

"I don't care if I have. I'm not afraid of her." If Mam had had Granny's skill, she'd have known I was indeed scared of the old woman. I knew full well I should have been polite, but my tongue had a way of getting away from me. I said what I thought and didn't think about the consequences until it was too late.

Now, far from Granny's prying eyes, I held the necklace up and watched it sparkle in the sunlight. "You want me to wear this, don't you?" I asked Thomas. "That's why you gave it to me."

He smiled so widely, I saw the buds of new teeth pushing up through his pink gums. Surely Thomas wouldn't come to harm if I wore the necklace for just a few moments. With care I undid the clasp and fastened the chain around my neck. How beautiful it was.

I should have given the necklace back to Thomas, but instead I tucked it inside my dress. I liked the smooth feel of the locket against my skin. Just for a little while, I thought. What harm could come to Thomas with me so near?

It seemed at least a dozen thistles had sprouted while my back was turned. Their thorny stems hurt my hands, and their roots held the soil tightly. I tugged and tugged until my back hurt from bending over. If I did much more weeding, I'd be an old woman before I even grew up. I'd hobble around in ragged clothes and end up as crazy as Granny Hedgepath.

While I worked, a large cloud drifted across the sun and plunged the garden into its shadow. At the same time, the breeze dropped and a strange silence fell. No leaves rustled.

Chickens stopping clucking and disappeared into their coop. No birds sang. No bees hummed in the clover. The colors of flowers and grass, trees and sky faded to gray.

Worried, I got to my feet to check on Thomas. Suddenly the world seemed to spin and lurch. Colors blurred and ran together. I saw two of everything. The sky was beneath me, the grass above me. Too dizzy to stand, I fell to the ground. The last thing I heard was a crow laughing.